And suddenly, chaos . . .

The noise of the explosion hit Will full force, and pain stabbed at his eardrums. Although he didn't actually stagger, he felt as if the planet had suddenly tilted, stealing his sense of balance.

When he had recovered, he stood very still, his mouth open, his dark eyes wide as he watched the lower half of the stone Science building collapse in upon itself like an accordion. The outside walls of the first and second floor disappeared, crumbling into a gray cloud of shattered stone.

MED CENTER

MED CENTER™

DIANE HOH

SCHOLASTIC INC.
New York Toronto London Auckland Sydney

ISBN 0-590-67317-3

12 11 10 9 8 7 6 5 4 3 2 1   6 7 8 9/9 0 1/0

Printed in the U.S.A.   01

First Scholastic printing, November 1996

MED CENTER ™

blast

prologue

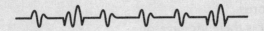

Some of the chemicals arrive in fat, squat bottles, like gallons of vinegar or photo developing fluid. The bottles are wrapped in thick layers of brown paper, as if their contents should remain a secret, although these particular chemicals arrive daily at the back entrance to the Science building on the campus of Grant University. They are commonly used in chemistry classes everywhere and are thickly wrapped not for secrecy's sake, but to protect the wide, deep boxes they come in from spillage should a bottle break in transit. Some of the stronger chemicals could eat through thick cardboard in seconds.

Some of the chemicals are packed in tins or canisters or plastic bags.

Under the right circumstances, the chemicals are relatively harmless. Still, their labels read, DANGER. CHEMICALS. USE WITH CAUTION.

The word *caution* should never be ignored. It is there for a reason. In this case, it could mean, "Do not use these chemicals without adequate supervision." And it could mean, "Do not mix one compound with another except under the watchful eye of a qualified chemist." It could mean, "No matter how curious you might be, do not experiment willy-nilly."

The word *caution* in this case should not be ignored.

It is there for a reason.

chapter

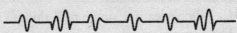

Abby O'Connor hugged her emerald green ski jacket tightly around her against the icy January night as she and her best friend, Susannah Grant, hurried across the campus of Grant University. The lighted walkways were busy with students and professors hurrying along, anxious to escape the cold.

Abby and Susannah had just finished a refresher course in first aid, a class required for their volunteer duties at Med Center. The huge medical complex, comprised of eighteen brick buildings in varying sizes, was located on property adjacent to Grant University. "Didn't we already know all that stuff?" Abby asked through lips numb with cold. "I gave up a nice, cozy evening at home in front of a warm fireplace, or better yet, an evening with Sid, just to go over the same things we learned in our hospital volunteer classes last summer. What a waste of time! And how come Kate wasn't there?"

"Because she took the course last week." Susannah's pale hair was tucked up underneath a thick, white knit cap that matched the lining of her suede jacket. Her lovely oval face was red with cold, her bright blue eyes sparkling. "If we want to keep volunteering, we have to take it every six months, remember?"

"Well, I didn't learn a single new thing," said Abby. She was shorter than Susannah by half a foot, and had to walk very fast to keep up with her. The effort made Abby's voice husky, as if she had a slight cold. "Except I'd forgotten the term for a patient coughing up blood, and I didn't remember what a fainting episode was called."

"See? That's why we need these courses. We forget things." Susannah smiled at Abby. "Things like bloody *emesis* and *syncope*."

"*You* don't."

"Of course I do." Susannah ran down a set of stone steps and held open the door to one of the many coffee bars scattered around campus. Most of them, like this one, were situated in basements, in spaces that formerly had been used only for storage. Then four enterprising students had decided that what Grant University really needed — and wanted — was more coffee. They were right, and the small, informal cafés had proved very popular.

Warmth, noise, and the inviting odor of vanilla-flavored coffee wafted out to draw Susannah and Abby inside. "I just think it's great," Susannah said, "that the university lets high school volunteers sit in on the refresher courses for free. They could charge us tuition, and they don't."

"Like you have to worry about that," Abby pointed out, shaking free of her hood and running a hand through carelessly arranged dark curls. There was amusement in her round, pretty face and thickly lashed dark eyes as she added, "Your father practically *owns* the university, Sooz. Not to mention everything else in the city of Grant, Massachusetts." It still surprised her occasionally that her best friend lived in a mansion, while Abby herself lived in a sprawling but slightly worn ranch house with her parents, a grandfather, several pets, and five siblings. Although the house was always clean, it was inevitably cluttered, and her mother sometimes complained mildly that she spent every waking moment wiping away peanut butter handprints or muddy footprints. Linden Hall, where Susannah lived with her parents and her twin brother, Sam, was three times the size of the O'Connor home. The floors were sparkling marble or pristine white carpeting. And the expensive antique furniture was *totally* free of peanut butter. There was no similarity between the two households whatsoever.

The weird thing was that Susannah, whose gorgeous suite on the second floor of Linden Hall consisted of three beautifully decorated rooms, spent far more time at the O'Connor home than she did at her own. Her parents led an active social life and were seldom home, and Sam was equally busy dating, partying, or participating in an athletic event.

Abby had to admit, the mansion probably wouldn't be such a great place to be if you were the only person within its thick stone walls. Maybe you'd feel like the sole occupant of a deserted fortress. Grim.

It seemed to Abby that Susannah felt the same way.

"Well, Kate doesn't have money," Susannah reminded Abby. "I know *she* was relieved to find out the classes didn't cost anything." She took off her coat, stamped her booted feet to warm them, and glanced around the small, bustling café, completely unaware of the interested looks sent in her direction. In white leggings and a white tunic sweater that accentuated her slenderness, her face flushed from the cold, she made a pleasing picture as she pulled the white cap off and set her long, wavy hair free to settle around her shoulders. Her eyes swept the packed café. "Anyone here we know?"

Abby grinned. "You mean like Will Jackson? He's on paramedic duty tonight, remember?"

"Why would I be looking for Will? I told you, he's mad at me." Susannah sighed, remembering the argument. She and Will Jackson, a paramedic at Grant Memorial Hospital, had planned to take in a movie at the mall the night before. It would have been their first real date, and she'd been really excited about it. Apparently, Will had finally reached the point where he was willing to brave the stares sure to come when Grant residents spotted him arm in arm with Susannah Grant. Samuel Grant II's daughter with *Will Jackson*? The same Will Jackson who didn't have a penny to his name? Who drove a truck instead of a Lexus or a Miata? Who lived in Eastridge, along with most of the other African-American residents of Grant? Now *there* was a match that was sure to cause more than a few heads to turn.

Susannah didn't care what people thought. As for her parents, the people Will was most worried about, he could relax. No matter what they thought, Samuel Grant II and his wife, Caroline, would never dare say anything rude when Will came to pick her up. For one thing, they were both too civilized. To Susannah's parents, the importance of good manners ranked right up there with the importance of good, sound financial investments. It would take more than Will Jackson to make them lose their cool. And for another thing, the Grants were both active in liberal organizations all over the city. It would have been too hypocritical of them to express disapproval when they saw Susannah with Will. Her father, for all of his other faults, claimed he hated hypocrisy. She liked to believe that he meant it.

But Will never came to Linden Hall. Yesterday afternoon, Susannah casually had suggested first that they take her car, a silver Mercedes-Benz convertible, in order to save Will gas money, and second, that she pay for the movie tickets. She thought she was just being considerate. He thought she was being patronizing, and he told her so. Then he'd stormed out of the ER. So much for their first date.

She knew the whole thing was her fault. Who knew more about Will's stiff-necked pride than she did? How could she have been stupid enough to treat him as if he were a charity case? No wonder he'd gone ballistic.

She hadn't seen him since, but in a way, that was a relief. She hadn't a clue about what she'd say to him. A simple "I'm sorry" probably wouldn't cut it.

"There's Jeremy," Abby said, pointing. "Over there with Callie Matthews." She groaned. "Lately it seems like everywhere I turn, Callie is there. Ever since she saved Carmel's life during the flood, she acts like I owe her, big time. It was my *sister's* life she saved, not mine. Why doesn't she go hang around *Carmel*?"

"Because Carmel's only eight, and Callie's seventeen."

Abby glowered. "Sounds like a perfect match to me, considering Callie's maturity level."

"You're insulting Carmel." Susannah was no

fan of Callie Matthews, either. The girl was just plain mean. Callie's father was the hospital's chief administrator and she never let anyone forget it. She was one of the people in Grant sure to make life miserable for Susannah and Will, if they ever *did* get around to publicly dating.

Abby followed Susannah over to the small, round table in the middle of the room where Jeremy Barlow sat with Callie. They were elbow-to-elbow with people sitting at other small, round tables, sipping coffee and reading or studying.

"I didn't know you hung out here, Jeremy," Susannah said, sending Callie a nonchalant wave. "Trying to see what it'll feel like to be a student at Grant U?"

"*I* won't be going here," Callie interjected with disdain. Callie Matthews was tiny, with far too much thick, blonde hair for someone so small. There was a petulant downturn to her mouth. She was wearing, as she often did, bright red from head to toe. Even her boots were red. "My father," she continued, "says only an Ivy League college is suitable for someone with my grades and talent."

"Susannah wasn't talking to *you*," Abby said flatly. "She was talking to Jeremy. But we are devastated to learn that you won't be attending Grant with us, aren't we, Susannah? This is a *major* blow."

Callie frowned and focused her attention on

Susannah instead. "Susannah, *you're* not really thinking of coming *here* to college, are you? I can't believe your parents will let you. I mean, they could afford to send you anywhere in the world! Why would you want to settle for dinky old Grant University?"

Shrugging, Susannah replied, "Grant isn't so dinky. It has what I want, which is a great premed program. And it happens to be right next door to the largest, most respected medical complex in the country. Why would I want to go anywhere else?"

Abby went to get their coffee. Ignoring Callie's response, Susannah repeated her question to Jeremy. "Do you hang out here a lot?"

"Yeah, sometimes." Jeremy was nice-looking, with a square face and good bone structure, and thick, blonde hair that he wore very short, neatly parted, and heavily moussed into place. His smile softened his angular features, but Jeremy didn't smile easily. "They have sandwiches here, so when my dad's not coming home for dinner, I can get something to eat with my coffee. I like the atmosphere, and I've met some okay people."

Susannah nodded. Thomas Barlow, Jeremy's dad, was the chief cardiologist at Grant Memorial. He was a very busy, very important man, and probably not home very much. Jeremy's mother had walked out the door and left for San Francisco to become a writer. Jeremy's huge, stone home must seem cavernous to him now. Susannah knew exactly how that felt. No wonder he had taken to hanging out someplace where he was sure to find plenty of people.

"In fact," Jeremy continued, his solemn face unusually animated, "I met this cool guy here. He's really interesting. Some kind of scientific genius, I guess, the way he talks about chemistry and biology and earth sciences, all that stuff. I never liked science much myself, but he has this way of making it seem exciting. He's got me thinking about maybe becoming a medical researcher. That way, my old man would get off my back about my becoming a doctor, and I'd get to work in a nice, quiet laboratory somewhere."

Susannah knew why Jeremy never had cared much about science. Or pretended not to. It was because his father was constantly pushing him to go into medicine, and Jeremy couldn't stand the thought. If there was one thing Jeremy did *not* want to do, it was follow in his father's footsteps. He didn't want the kind of attention his famous father got. Unlike Callie Matthews, who craved attention of any kind, Jeremy wasn't a spotlight seeker. A laboratory would give him the peace and quiet he wanted.

"This guy's name is Tim Beech," Jeremy continued enthusiastically, "and he's conducting experiments on something that just might give

11

people more energy, keep them from ever getting tired. Isn't that wild? I'm supposed to meet him at the science building in" — he glanced at his expensive gold watch. "Damn, I'm late! Want to come along? You might learn something."

Callie looked interested and moved to stand up. Susannah shook her head and said, "I can't. I'm meeting Sam here. We're having dinner with the parents at Riverside Lodge. Thanks, anyway."

At the mention of Sam's name, and the news that he was about to appear, Callie sank back into her seat so quickly, her chair trembled. If there was even the tiniest chance that Sam would invite Callie Matthews along on this family outing, she wasn't budging. Recently, Sam had been dating a gymnast named Margo Porter. Since Sam never stuck to one girl for any length of time, Callie hadn't given up hope. One of these days, Sam would look at her and see how much more they could have together than their occasional, *very* fun dates. That hadn't happened yet, but it still could. She wasn't about to miss an opportunity to be with Sam, not for some stupid science experiment.

When Jeremy had departed, Callie mused aloud, "Sam isn't bringing that gymnast, is he? If you're going out to dinner, taking her with you would be a waste of time. She looks like one of those people who eat nothing but vegetables, until they finally start to look like one. I've seen celery sticks that looked healthier than Margo Porter."

Susannah wasn't listening. She was thinking about Will, wondering if he was ever going to speak to her again. And wondering what she would do if he didn't.

In the Science building, Jeremy hurried down a hallway on the second floor, trying to remember which room Tim Beech had said he'd be in. Two twenty-five? Twenty-six? He should have written it down.

Two guys in sweat clothes, one carrying a basketball, were coming toward Jeremy in the hallway. "Excuse me," he asked quickly, "do either of you guys know Tim Beech?"

One of the boys laughed. "Dr. Jekyll? Sure. Everybody knows the mad scientist." He motioned over his shoulder. "He's back there in two twenty-seven, concocting another weird cocktail. If I were you, I'd steer clear of him. You don't want to be around when he drinks that stuff and turns into Mr. Hyde." Laughing, the two boys walked away.

Jeremy frowned. Wasn't Tim the genius that he'd seemed to be? Maybe they just didn't understand Tim's dedication to science. Some people didn't get things like that.

In the doorway of room two twenty-seven, which was a well-equipped, well-lit chemistry laboratory, Jeremy hesitated. Tim was sitting alone at a table in the center of the room. Armed with half a dozen glass beakers, four of which held frothing, steamy concoctions, and two lit Bunsen burners, he sat with his eyes focused on the steaming beakers, completely oblivious to his surroundings. There were two other students in the room, and a teaching assistant. The students, engaged in conversation, were standing near a shelf of books at the rear of the lab. The TA was writing chemical equations on the blackboard up front.

It wasn't as if there was a class going on. Still, it didn't seem right to Jeremy to interrupt Tim's deep concentration. But, Tim *had* invited him. And now that he was actually thinking about becoming a medical researcher, maybe even one day finding a cure for the HIV virus or for cancer, he was anxious to learn more about the field.

Calling out Tim's name, Jeremy moved on into the room.

chapter
2

In Grant High's gymnasium, Sam Grant III stood in the bleachers glancing impatiently at his watch. He was supposed to pick up Susannah at The Beanery at nine, and it was already quarter past eight. Margo had just begun her balance beam routine. When she finished, she'd have to shower and change. How long would that take?

He shouldn't have asked her along tonight. The invitation had been an impulse, which was not at all unusual for him. She'd been feeling down about her family situation, and he'd felt sorry for her. But now he was annoyed with himself, because what he'd really been planning to do was cool it with Margo. They really didn't have that much in common. They were both athletes, but that was about it, he'd discovered. And Margo Porter wasn't looking very much like an athlete these days. The strain at home had taken some pounds off her. He'd been avoiding her lately, and hadn't realized until tonight, when she ran out onto the floor in her blue leotard, just how much weight she'd lost. She was awfully

15

thin. If she'd looked like this six months ago, he never would have asked her out in the first place.

Waiting for her to finish was screwing up his schedule. They were meeting his parents, and his father, Samuel Grant II, considered tardiness a sign of weak character.

Sam began tapping his foot impatiently to the music accompanying Margo's routine. She loved the balance beam, she'd told him. And she was very good at it, putting her all into every move she made.

Telling himself to relax, Sam focused his attention on the small, thin girl standing on her hands on the narrow balance beam. The things the team did on that small piece of equipment, with so little space for maneuvering, always amazed him. Margo, in particular, was well known for her ability to do so much with so little.

He knew her routine. She was almost finished. Good. He'd have to urge her to rush through her shower. Better to have slightly damp hair than to be late for a dinner with his parents.

Sam started down the bleachers, intending to wait for Margo at the exit from the gym. So he didn't see exactly what happened. All he knew for sure was, one second she was dancing lightly, perfectly balanced, toward one end of the beam, and the next second there was a collective, horrified gasp from the spectators. When he looked up, there was a crumpled heap of blue lying at the base of the balance beam, and coaches and teammates were rushing toward it.

Margo had fallen.

She quickly sat up, her face strained, her eyes huge. She had never fallen in competition before, not once, and she was stunned. She began crying then, holding her right arm against her chest like a broken wing.

Oh, great, he thought involuntarily. Then, ashamed of himself, he ran to the fallen girl's side.

In Emergency Services at Grant Memorial Hospital, Will Jackson had just finished explaining to Kate Thompson why he'd been in such a rotten mood all evening. It had been a quiet, peaceful night. He should have been relaxed, but the argument he'd had with Susannah had left a bitter taste in his mouth, and a knot in his stomach.

"You're a reactionary, Will," Kate said matter-of-factly when Will had told her about the argument. They were close friends. Will was much more likely to tell Kate about his problems than any of his many male friends. She was a better listener, and she always told the truth. They'd grown up in Eastridge together, attended the same high school, and knew each other well. "You react to everything so fast, before you think about it. Susannah was just trying to be thoughtful. You know that's how she is."

There were people, especially at the hospital, who thought because Kate and Will were the same age, came from the same neighborhood, were both African-Americans, and both intended to go into medicine one day, they should get together romantically. Will had thought about that possibility, too, off and on, though he'd never gotten around to pursuing the idea. Then, one day last year, Susannah Grant had walked into the ER in her pink volunteer's smock, her sun-colored hair pulled away from her face in one of those French braid things, and smiled at him. And that was that.

Will already knew Sam. They'd competed in plenty of athletic events. Will liked Sam, although he thought the Grant heir was a little spoiled.

It didn't take him long to figure out that Susannah wasn't anything like Sam. She had fixed those incredibly bright blue eyes on him when Kate introduced them, smiled a friendly smile, and extended her hand. He'd been bowled over and hadn't recovered yet. The more time he spent around her, the more he realized what a difficult position she was in as Samuel Grant II's only daughter. She seemed to waver between the confidence that came along with money and position, and the uncertainty created by never knowing if people liked you *because* of that money and position, or for yourself. So many times, he'd thought they were growing closer, in spite of the obstacles against that happening, and he'd allowed his hopes to rise. Every time, something happened that told him he'd been wrong. He could almost *see* her pulling away again. And, to be honest, he often pulled away, too.

"You *do* know that's how she is?" Kate repeated. Susannah and Kate had been the only two high school students to pass a series of tests that allowed them entry into Med Center's ER as volunteers. Once Kate had gotten over the initial shock of working with someone so privileged, she had grown to like and respect Susannah. Staff members, afraid of offending Samuel Grant's daughter or making a mistake in front of her, still kept her at arm's length. But Kate and her mother, Astrid, ER's head nurse, refused to let Susannah's social status get in the way. Kate had watched with amusement as Will melted under Susannah's genuine warmth. Now, she was convinced that he was falling in love with her.

Kate also believed the feeling was mutual. She could see it in Susannah's eyes whenever she looked at Will. But Kate Thompson wasn't holding her breath until either one of them admitted their feelings. They were both cautious, it seemed to her, at least where feelings were concerned. And then there was Will's pride . . . the cause of this, their first real argument. She knew how Will saw it: Susannah had everything, he had nothing.

"She knows you're broke most of the time," Kate pressed on. "And she's *not*, so it made sense to her to suggest picking up the tab." An orderly in green passed them pushing an empty gurney, and two student nurses in white entered the lounge. Kate lowered her voice. "You're a reverse snob, that's what you are, Will Jackson. Susannah, on the other hand, doesn't have a snobbish bone in her body. She is *not* a princess, Will, so quit expecting her to act like one."

Tall, lanky Will, his navy blue paramedic's jacket draped over one arm, leaned against the wall and nodded, his handsome, sharply angled face serious. "I know. You're right. I overreacted. It's just that I'd put the bucks aside for our date. I *wanted* to pay."

Kate's model-perfect, oval face eased into a knowing grin. "Me Tarzan, you helpless female? Me pay, you eternally grateful? Gimme a break, Will, it's almost the twenty-first century! Anyway, Susannah is *always* going to be rich. You'll probably still be poor when you're a doctor because you're planning to open a clinic in Eastridge. That is *not* the way to fame and fortune, we both know that. So you'd better swallow that silly pride of yours and get used to Susannah shelling out a dollar here, a dollar there, if you want any kind of future with her. I don't see why *she* should have to pretend to be poor just because you are."

Will considered Kate's words for a minute, then asked, "You know where she is now?"

"Um-hum, I do, but I don't think I should tell you. You haven't suffered enough yet."

"Kate!"

"Oh, all right. She and O'Connor took the refresher course tonight. But you'd better hurry up if you want to catch her at the university, because she and Sam have plans to go out to dinner with Mama and Papa Grant tonight. Sam's picking her up at the coffee bar closest to the nursing school. It's in the basement of that building right beside the Science building. You know the one?"

Will nodded. "Yeah. The Math building. The coffee bar is called The Beanery."

"Well, that's where she is." Kate gave Will a gentle push. "Go on if you're going. Don't forget to clock out first. I'll tell Astrid you're taking your break. But hurry up. Susannah said Sam was picking her up at nine, and it's almost nine now."

Looking far more cheerful than he had a few minutes earlier, Will jogged out of the building.

He hadn't been gone more than a minute or two when the wail of an ambulance died at the rear entrance. Kate turned and hurried to join the medical team waiting in the cold under the canopy just beyond the door.

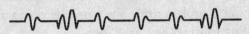

Kate was surprised to see Samuel Grant jump from his silver van before the ambulance doors opened. Susannah and Sam were not identical twins. Sam was taller than Susannah, his face narrower. But he had the same blonde hair, the same cobalt blue eyes. "I'm with her," he said to Kate, gesturing toward the emergency vehicle. "I was in the gym when she fell. I wanted to make sure she's okay. Will my van be towed if I leave it here?"

The van was new, silver, like Susannah's Benz. "No, they'll give you a few minutes. Then you'll have to move it to the parking garage over there." Kate pointed to a tall, gray stone structure across the way.

Sam nodded and turned his attention to the doors being yanked open at the rear of the ambulance.

While the patient was being lifted out, Sam quickly explained what had happened. "She hasn't been feeling so hot lately," he added, and asked the paramedic administering oxygen to the patient how she was doing.

"Vital signs are good," he said as they shifted the fully conscious, but silent girl to the waiting gurney and hurried her into the hospital. "It looks like a broken arm. She won't be doing any tumbling routines any time soon."

Kate shot him a disapproving look. The girl was conscious. They weren't supposed to say things like that if there was any chance that the patient could overhear.

"Margo?" she asked, peering down into the girl's face. The skin was pallid, the eyes encircled with bluish hollows, the cheekbones so prominent, they looked as if they had been sculpted from rock. "Margo, how are you feeling?"

She got no answer. The girl turned her head away. With her uninjured arm, she pulled the white blanket up to her chin.

She sure doesn't look like an athlete, Kate thought as they rolled the gurney to a treatment room. She looks sick, and that couldn't be just from the fall. Maybe she fell *because* she's sick. Why didn't someone notice and keep her off that balance beam? Why didn't *Sam* notice? Or her parents?

Sam wasn't happy about being forced to wait in the waiting room, but Kate insisted. He wasn't related to the girl. "If you want to be helpful," she said, "call her parents. They should be here."

Dr. Cathy Shumann, a short, round, perennially cheerful resident, completed a quick check to make sure Margo had no head or chest injury. Then she asked Astrid and Kate to cut off the patient's clothing so she could examine her torso and limbs. It was after they had done so that Kate began to suspect what the real problem was.

When the pale blue leotard had been cut away and Margo's upper body was exposed, Kate, Astrid, and Dr. Shumann all stared in dismay. The small ribs jutted upward so sharply that with every breath the girl took, it seemed the bones might pierce through the pale, bluish skin like the spokes of a broken umbrella.

She's been starving herself, Kate thought with sickening certainty. Was Margo suffering from anorexia? Kate had seen other cases. There had been two since she began her volunteer work at Memorial. One girl had been only eleven years old, the other eighteen. They had both been in such bad shape by the time they were admitted, they were immediately taken to ICU. But even in the Intensive Care Unit, there was only so much the medical staff could do. The older girl had died. The eleven-year-old girl was still an outpatient at Med Center's Psych building. Kate had seen her occasionally, going in and coming out. She hadn't looked as if she'd gained much weight. But she hadn't looked any thinner, either, so maybe she was holding her own.

Margo, in pain from the broken arm, but acutely aware that she was being stared at, and why, snatched at the sheet and yanked it upward. Tears rolled down her gaunt face, but she made no sound, and she said nothing.

"She's a gymnast," Kate murmured. She knew the leotard had already told *that* story. She said it, anyway, because she felt it might have something to do with Margo's condition. One of the girls who'd been in ICU had been a gymnast, with Olympic aspirations. She had entered competition at the age of eight, when she was very tiny. But when puberty struck, she began filling out. The changes in her body, though they were perfectly normal, frightened her. She became terrified of losing her dream. Keeping her weight down had become the most important thing in her life. That girl was only eighteen when she died.

Dr. Shumann let out a concerned sigh. Then she very quickly finished her exam. When she was done, she ordered, "Call Orthopedics. When the arm has been taken care of, get her upstairs to ICU and get some fluids into her. Get *something* into her!" She stripped off her rubber gloves. Saying grimly, "As for me, I'm so interested in hearing what her parents have to say about how she managed to put herself in this condition, *I'm* going to call them myself," she marched from the room, leaving Kate no opportunity to say the parents had already been called. *If* Sam had remembered to call them, that is.

A small, defeated sob escaped Margo. "My mother's going to kill me," she whispered, keeping her face turned away from Kate. "She's had so much on her mind lately, she didn't notice for a long time. Then, when she did, she kept nagging at me to eat. I started wearing lots of layers of clothing around the house so she'd leave me alone."

You couldn't wear clothes over your face, Kate wanted to say. *Didn't your mother see what was happening to your face?* She stopped herself in time. Margo was already very upset. And very sick, although she probably wouldn't admit that. She might not even be aware of it. People suffering from eating disorders, Kate had learned last summer, almost never accepted that they were ill. And they often became very angry when other people hinted that they *were*. Other people looked at anorexics and saw skin and bones, but *they* looked into a mirror and saw fat. Kate couldn't understand that. It made no sense.

She held Margo's hand and talked to her quietly while the Ortho man worked on the broken arm. Margo, who had been mildly sedated, was silent the entire time. She never made a sound.

In the Science building, Jeremy had obeyed Tim Beech's strict order to "Be quiet and just watch. Don't hassle me, okay? Take a seat there and watch genius at work."

But Jeremy was getting bored. He didn't understand what Tim was doing, and the idea of becoming a medical researcher was rapidly fading. Jeremy liked *people*, though they didn't always like him back, and the thought of spending hours alone on a stool in a quiet, isolated lab already had begun to lose its appeal. While he had no desire to be as well known as his father, neither did he want to disappear from the world entirely, which seemed to be what Tim Beech was doing. Hunched over the table with its sink and faucets, its Bunsen burners glowing blue, Tim seemed totally unaware of the world around him as he poured frothy mixtures from one beaker to another. He never once looked up, and after that first direct order to Jeremy, didn't say another word.

This is not for me, Jeremy thought, and stood up. He hesitated, unsure whether or not he should even say good-bye. Deciding Tim wouldn't hear him if he did, he turned and began walking to the door.

Behind him, he heard as clearly as if Tim had said it directly into his ear, "Uh-oh."

Then the room exploded in a blinding flash of light and an ear-shattering, thunderous roar.

chapter

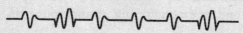

The force of the blast next door rocked the Math building. In the basement coffee bar, tables tilted sideways, or bounced up into the air. Chairs tipped over, spilling their occupants onto the tile floor. The few empty chairs skidded across the room as if they had wheels. Steaming, dark brown liquid from machines and pots spewed everywhere, scalding bare arms, the backs of necks, and several faces. Cries of pain and shock sounded, then were drowned out by the lengthy, rumbling roar of the explosion.

A waitress on her way to a table, a tray of filled mugs in her hand, was struck in the back of the head by a flying coffeepot. The blow knocked her to the floor. Her tray shot up into the air and sailed across the room to slam into the cracked front window. The coffeepot exploded on impact, sending a shower of glass out into the room. People who hadn't been tossed to the floor threw themselves down voluntarily, shielding their heads with their hands.

The lights went out.

When all sound and motion ceased, everyone stayed where they were, too stunned and frightened to move. Tables and chairs were scattered everywhere, some overturned, some lying on top of prone bodies, others tilted up on only two legs, leaning against a wall or the counter. Shattered mugs, crumpled paper napkins, spoons, and tiny blue and white and pink packets of sugar littered the floor like confetti. Much of the debris had been splattered with brown liquid.

The noise of the blast finally died with one last grumble that mimicked the distant thunder of a waning storm.

But there was no storm.

Too shocked and stunned to feel fear, Susannah lay where she was, amid a jumble of overturned chairs and tangled arms and legs. Trying to comprehend what had happened, her first thought was, earthquake. Other voices echoed the thought aloud. But even as the voices registered, Susannah dismissed the probability. The city of Grant, Massachusetts, occasionally suffered some really miserable weather. But as far as she knew, it had never experienced an earthquake.

A sudden, breathless silence fell. During the long, dead moment when all sight and sound faded, it seemed to Susannah that time itself had stopped.

Then Abby's husky voice floated out of the

darkness. "What *was* it? What's happened?"

Someone cried, "Earthquake!" but another voice quickly disagreed. "No way! It had to be an explosion. Anyone smell smoke?"

Susannah did. Others did, too. The thought of fire in such crowded, chaotic surroundings filled the room with panic. How could they save themselves from fire when it was too dark to see? Someone groaned in pain. "I've been burned!" a male voice cried. "My face, my neck . . . they feel like they're on fire!"

"It's so dark, I can't tell where the door is!" Callie cried. She sounded panic-stricken, her voice higher and thinner than usual.

"The door is where it *always* was," Abby said shakily. And then, realizing that she couldn't be sure that was true, she added in an abashed voice, "At least, it probably is. Anyway, I don't think there's a fire in here. The smell of smoke isn't getting any stronger, and it's so dark in here, we'd see flames right away if there were any. If there *is* a fire, it must be next door. In the Science building."

"Well, that's *too* close," Callie protested. "If there *was* an explosion over there and there's a fire, it'll spread to us really fast. We've got to get out of here!"

People climbed to their feet and began surging toward the door. In the pitch-black, Susannah couldn't see them, but she was in the middle of the room and could feel the floor beneath her vibrating with approaching feet. A foot collided with her outstretched ankle. She stood up hastily, brushing at her hair and clothing, and was nearly knocked off balance by someone pushing past her.

A welcome glow of light appeared suddenly from the counter, which stood to the right of the door. "Don't panic!" one of the waitresses called, holding aloft a lighted candle. Her voice effectively halted the noisy stampede as people glanced toward the source of the light. "Wait until you can see better, or someone's going to get hurt. We have more candles here. Anyway," she added as she lit two more candles and placed them on the counter, "maybe you shouldn't go out there until we know what's happened. You don't know what's going on."

Buoyed by even that minimal break in the darkness, the crowd stopped pushing. Susannah and Abby quickly moved to the counter to ask for clean napkins, which they then wet at the sink and passed out to soothe scalded skin.

Stepping carefully to avoid unseen, broken shards of glass, a boy in a gray Grant University sweatshirt pressed his face up against the spider-webbed glass of the splintered window. "I can't see a thing," he complained. "There are no lights out there anywhere."

"The electricity must be off in the whole

area," the waitress said. She was bleeding from a small cut on her forehead. She pressed a white napkin against it as she spoke. "Something really bad must have happened." She left the counter to go to the aid of the other waitress, just now scrambling to her feet, clearly dazed from the blow to the back of her head.

No one argued with the expression "something really bad" had happened. The force with which the coffee bar had been affected had already given them that news. They stood silently, disbelief in their eyes, staring at the candles on the counter, unsure of what to do next, or if they should do anything at all.

At Med Center, the full shock of the blast was tempered by the five-block distance. Even then, all eighteen of the buildings felt the effect. Hallway lights in the Psych Building flickered nervously, bringing cries of alarm from patients' rooms. Bottles of pills careened off shelves in the Rehab Hospital. Medical charts in the Oncology building banged violently against patients' beds. At Grant Memorial, the reverberation of the explosion echoed from the basement to the top floors.

On the tenth floor, Callie's father, Caleb Matthews, jerked upright in his leather chair and shouted into his luxurious, empty office, "What the hell was *that*?"

Ambulance attendants who were bringing in two young boys suffering from smoke inhalation staggered under the force of the explosion, but never lost their grip on their stretchers. Their reaction was identical to that of Caleb Matthews, and their voices echoed his startled cry.

Astrid Thompson, taking a much-needed break in the ER staff lounge, heard the distant rumbling sound and felt a slight tremor in the room. She lunged, in vain, for the glass tumbler full of orange juice that she had just placed on the wooden arm of the old tweed couch. Her aim was off. The glass dove for the white tile floor and hit it hard, shattering into a mess of glass shards and orange pulp.

Reaching for a roll of paper towels sitting on the sink ledge, she murmured, "What on earth . . . ?"

Upstairs in ICU, Margo Porter heard the distant roar and watched with bewildered eyes as the IV bag hanging above her rocked back and forth, slapping against its pole like a flag caught in a brisk wind. She was too weak to call for a nurse, so she lay there quietly with her eyes on the plastic bag, wondering what was happening.

Sam jumped to his feet in the ICU waiting room. He had narrowly escaped drowning in a recent flood in Grant, and his dismayed comment when the pictures on the hallway walls began dancing was, "Oh, man, what *now*?"

Kate, waiting just inside the double glass doors for the two young patients, heard the ear-shattering roar and clapped her hands against her ears. She half expected the canopy over the entrance to come crashing down around her, crushing the ambulance, the paramedics, and the patients, as well as the doctor and nurse standing next to them. But the canopy remained in place as the booming sound faded. When silence fell, no one said anything. They were still waiting for something more to happen.

Will Jackson was loping along one of the University's walkways toward the coffee bar when the ground beneath his feet suddenly began to tremble. He had been concentrating so studiously on what he was going to say to Susannah to patch things up, his first thought at his loss of equilibrium was that he had stumbled on an uneven spot in the sidewalk. Then the noise of the explosion hit him full force, and pain stabbed at his eardrums. Although he didn't actually stagger, he felt as if the planet had suddenly tilted, stealing his sense of balance.

When he had recovered, he stood very still, his mouth open, his dark eyes wide as he watched the lower half of the stone Science building collapse in upon itself like an accordion. The outside walls of the first and second floor disappeared, crumbling into a gray cloud of shattered stone. Every supporting beam toppled, and the entire second floor fell straight down to the first floor. The resulting collision sent up so much dust and smoke, it was impossible to see if the third floor remained intact.

Shocked to the core, Will had only one thought: The building being destroyed in front of his eyes stood shoulder-to-shoulder with the Math building. The Math building contained The Beanery, and The Beanery contained Susannah.

Taking a deep breath, Will broke into a run.

At the coffee bar, Abby pushed her way back to Susannah. "Are you okay?"

Gingerly examining a swelling on the back of her head, Susannah said, "I think so. We should go out and see what happened."

"I agree. We can't hide in here all night. Anyway, Callie's right about one thing. If the Science building is on fire, that's too close for comfort. We don't want to be trapped. Come on, let's get out of here."

Others followed them out. They left against the advice of the waitress, who urged them to wait for the police. They would, she said, certainly be arriving at any moment. But no one wanted to wait.

Stepping cautiously, some still holding wet napkins to their faces or necks, others walking carefully as if bruised, they all trailed silently out of the café into the icy January air. The sky above them was clear, the moon's silvery glow acting as a bright lamp.

Once they were outside, where the acrid smell of smoke hung heavy in the air, all eyes turned to the Science building.

chapter
5

Bathed in the moon's glow, the damage was clearly visible. People gasped in disbelief, others cried out, a few shouted in dismay. As the group from The Beanery cautiously made its way up the slope to get a closer look, students and teachers alike began to straggle out of surrounding buildings, drawn by curiosity. All were forced to step carefully, because every last trace of glass had been ripped from the windows of the damaged structure, and shards littered the grass around it.

Slowly, carefully, muttering in shock, the group continued on up the slope. The lawn was scattered with large and small chunks of stone from the building. Mixed in with the broken stone were pieces of paper, stalks of thick, white chalk, the glass of shattered beakers, books, backpacks, lab stools, coats, gloves, and bulletin boards with notes still attached to them. All of it was strewn haphazardly across the lawn, as if the building had suddenly become angry and tossed all of its contents out into the cold.

No one was really looking at the mess. All eyes

were focused on the building. Or what was left of it.

"Oh, my god," Abby breathed, "*look* at it!"

The outside walls of the first and second floors were gone, exposing the building's innards. The second floor had collapsed into the first. All that was left of the second floor ceiling, which they could see clearly, was a giant, gaping hole surrounded by jagged edges, like sharp teeth.

The beams supporting the third floor, revealed clearly by the absence of the second-floor ceiling, were still in place. But the center beam was cracked and sagging.

Although there were a few thin trails of black smoke rising from the first-floor mountain of refuse, there were no flames. And there were no screams, no cries for help. The only sounds were observers' shocked cries of disbelief.

A sudden movement off to Susannah's left caught her eye, pulling her gaze away from the scene. She saw an arm — in a blue sleeve — sticking out from beneath a large chunk of rock. The arm seemed to be pushing at the rock. A few feet away, a leg in jeans kicked futilely at the ground. The remainder of that figure was hidden, too, by layers of broken stone. Not far from that spot, Susannah saw two gloved hands waving frantically from beneath a slice of blackboard bearing white-chalked chemical equations.

Shouting, "There are *people* out here! They're hurt! We need *help*!" she broke into an awkward scramble over the litter to help.

Abby turned to go in search of a telephone. But as she did so, approaching sirens sounded in the distance, and instead, she struggled along with Susannah to reach the blue-jacketed arm.

A second or two later, fire trucks screeched to a halt in the street below the group standing at the base of the ruined building. A pair of ambulances was right behind them, followed by two police cars that slid to a halt on the avenue.

While Susannah, Abby, and several other people worked at dislodging the chunks of stone hiding the survivors of the blast, firemen began unrolling thick beige hoses.

"But there's no *fire*," Abby said, her voice still thickened with shock.

Two paramedics, bearing equipment, arrived, with two policemen right behind them. The four quickly assisted the efforts to remove the heaviest rubble from the injured. The first two people uncovered were wearing heavy coats, and had knit caps tilting sideways on their scratched and bleeding heads.

"They have *coats* on," Abby said, standing back to let the paramedics tend to the injured. "They wouldn't have had coats on *inside* the building. These people must have been just passing by, Susannah. They got caught in the blast. So" — hope sounded in her voice — "maybe there *wasn't* anyone inside."

Susannah's eyes were bleak. Her face was red with cold, her hands shaking. "Abby, it's the Science building." Her voice, too, trembled with anxiety. "Unless Jeremy changed his mind at the last minute, *he* was in there."

There was a gush of air above them. When they looked up, scarlet flames had joined the smoke trailing thinly from the damaged building.

At Med Center, Sam stepped out of the elevator at ER and went looking for Kate. When he found her in a cubicle where the small victims of smoke inhalation were being treated, he beckoned to her. Frowning, she joined him in the hall. "I'm busy," she said quickly. "Did you find out what that horrible jolt was? I heard ambulances leaving here, but I haven't had a chance to ask anyone what's up."

Sam shook his head. "Not yet. It sounded like it came from campus. I have to go over there, anyway. I called my house to tell my parents about Margo and to cancel our dinner plans, but they'd already left. I'll have to catch them at The Beanery, I guess. While I'm over there, I'll see if anyone knows what's going on. Listen,

42

would you just keep an eye out for Margo? Run up to ICU and check on her once in a while?"

"I'll try. But I hardly know her, Sam. I'm sure she'd rather see you than me."

"They won't let me see her. You work here. They'll let you in. Anyway, I'll be right back. I just want to find out what's going on, and let my folks know where I'll be tonight."

Kate fixed a level gaze on Sam. "You don't have to stay with her, Sam. She *has* parents."

"I know. Maybe I'll just stay until they get here. I thought they'd be here by now, but . . ."

"Thompson!" the attending physician called impatiently. "This kid's about to heave again. Quit socializing and bring me a basin."

Sam was insistent. "Just check on her, okay?"

Kate nodded. "I'll try. Call here as soon as you find out something."

Sam agreed and hurried away.

Basin in hand, Kate returned to the patient not a moment too soon.

The two boys had been lucky. They had sneaked out of bed and were experimenting with matches in a shed behind their grandparents' house when they accidentally set the place on fire. Piles of old, damp newspapers had created so much smoke, the boys became disoriented and couldn't find the door. Fortunately for them, their grandfather had become suspicious and gone looking for them. He got them out before they suffered any serious burns.

Still, they were very ill, vomiting repeatedly, confused and dizzy. Kate felt sorry for both of them. They were only six and eight years old, and were no doubt in for a good tongue-lashing from either a grandparent or a parent, probably both.

She'd bet her favorite sneakers that this marked the end of their experimentation with flammable objects.

When she and an orderly had accompanied the boys to Pediatrics and they'd been tucked into their side-by-side beds, Kate headed for ICU to check on Sam's friend, Margo Porter.

Although Susannah and the others wanted desperately to help with the injured lying on the slope outside, firemen in yellow slickers ordered them away from the site. They reluctantly retreated to the sidewalk below to join the rapidly growing crowd gathered there. All watched with apprehension as thick, snakelike hoses were aimed on the flames.

Watching, Abby shivered and hugged herself. "I'll bet Jeremy isn't in there," she said, making a valiant effort to sound convincing. "There couldn't be *anyone* in there. I mean, they'd be shouting for help, wouldn't they?"

Not if they weren't able to, Susannah thought grimly, her eyes on the demolished lower floors. The shock had begun to ease somewhat, and she found herself thinking: An hour ago, Abby and I were walking by that building. If class had lasted just a little while longer, we could have been caught in the blast, too, just like those people scattered around on the ground up there.

The thought turned her palms clammy.

Someone called her name.

Susannah turned to see Will running straight toward her. The look in his eyes stopped her heart. When he reached her, breathing hard, he said nothing. He simply reached out and pulled her to him, clutching her tightly to his chest. Her face sank gratefully into the soft chill of his fleece-lined navy blue jacket. Unaware of anyone else around them, she wrapped her arms around him and silently hugged him back. She knew neither of them needed to say anything.

He held her for several moments, his chin resting on the top of her head. No one around them paid the slightest bit of attention. All eyes were on the fire-fighting efforts.

When he finally lifted his head, he said shakily, "Kate said you were in the coffee bar." He waved a hand. "The Beanery. It's so close. You could have been . . ."

"But I wasn't," she interrupted, reaching up to

gently touch his cheek. It was cold beneath her fingers. "We all got tossed around a little, but I don't think anyone was hurt."

He held her tightly again, murmuring into her hair, "You sure you're okay?"

"I'm okay. I promise."

Satisfied that she was all right, Will tore his gaze from her face and turned it toward the building. "What happened?"

"No one knows. An explosion of some kind, that's all we know so far. On the second floor. That floor is gone, so is the first. And the third floor isn't much better."

"The building was empty, right? I mean, it's late, so there shouldn't have been any classes."

"We don't know for sure that it *was* empty. Jeremy was with us in the coffee bar earlier, and he said he was coming here to meet someone. Some kid who was really into science. They might not have left before the explosion."

His eyes on the damaged structure, Will shook his head. "Oh, man, if he was in there . . ."

"Well, maybe he wasn't," Susannah added hastily. Will and Jeremy weren't really close friends, but they got along okay. "Abby's hoping he'd already left the building."

Will's eyes scanned the crowd. "If he'd left the building but was still hanging around campus, wouldn't he be here with us, wondering what was going on?"

Susannah didn't answer. She had been thinking the same thing.

"God," Will said softly, taking her hand in his and looking down at her, his eyes holding hers, "I'm glad you're okay. I was such a fool yesterday. All I could think about when I saw that building blow was, what if I never got the chance to explain."

"I wasn't hurt at all," she said. "But" — she pointed toward the injured — "other people weren't as lucky."

When Will saw what Susannah was pointing at, he drew in his breath sharply.

"I know you're itching to get over there and help," Susannah said quickly. "But the firemen have asked us to wait until the fire's out. They don't want anyone else getting hurt."

"If I was still on duty," Will said grimly, "I'd already be up there. But I clocked out right before I left Emsee. I can still help, though. How long do they expect us to wait before we can do something for those people?"

"I don't know."

They didn't have to wait long. As the last of the flames hissed into oblivion, the firemen began to withdraw their hoses. Will, Susannah, and Abby didn't even wait for a signal. They were already running up the slope to help. They were halfway there when Abby cried, "Look, there's someone coming out of the building!"

All heads turned. Bright moonlight revealed a figure staggering forth from a small door in the basement of the building. Hands to its head, it reeled from side to side, shouting something unintelligible.

The figure was wearing a dark-colored, bulky jacket.

The jacket was on fire.

chapter 6

The young man staggering out of the basement of the ruined building seemed unaware that the back of his bulky jacket was aflame. But as he left the building, the oxygen in the air fanned the fire, and everyone watched in horror as the flames reached for his uncovered head.

A fireman rushed to help. Will was right behind him. Together, they threw the young man on the ground and rolled him in the grass to kill the flames. Then they helped him to his feet and supported him between them to the ambulance. The crowd ran along behind the trio, anxious to see how the first survivor of the blast was.

"There are people in there," they heard the young man gasp. Will had stripped off the burned jacket and wrapped the victim in a blanket. He was attempting to administer oxygen, but the boy pushed the mask away. "I don't know how many people exactly," he said huskily. "They were in the science lab. I think that's where the explosion took place. And there was a girl in the science library with me. I don't know who she was, but she was still there when I left. You've got to get those people out. They have to be buried in there somewhere." He was seized then by a violent coughing spasm, and Will and another paramedic lifted him into the ambulance and put the oxygen mask over his face.

Will thrust his head out to tell Susannah, "I'm going back to Emsee with him. You coming?"

Susannah hesitated. If Jeremy was inside that mess, she wanted to be there for him when they brought him out. And there were all those people lying around outside, too. But she would be needed at Emergency when all of the victims were brought in.

Turning to Abby, she asked, "Are you staying?"

"Yeah, I think so. Maybe I can help out here. You go ahead with Will. Sid probably heard the explosion. He'll be coming over here to find out what happened. I'd like to be here when he comes."

Susannah had just stepped up into the ambulance when her brother's silver van screeched to a halt in front of the coffee bar. She waved to get his attention, and he ran over to her. Trying to take it all in at once — the crowd, the ruined building, the fire trucks and ambulances — he shook his head. "God, what happened? Susannah, are you okay?" Glancing again at the wreckage and noticing that she was inside the ambulance, he added, "You weren't *in* there, were you?"

"No." Will was tugging impatiently on Susannah's hand. "No, I was in the coffee bar, waiting for you. I'm okay. Look, Sam, I'm going back to Emsee. You'd better call Mom and Dad, make sure they know we're okay."

"They're not there. Probably on their way here."

"Well, when you see them, then. The fire's out in the building, but there are people outside *and* inside. Maybe you can help."

When the ambulance had pulled away, its siren wailing, Sam searched for Abby in the crowd. When he found her, he pushed his way through to stand at her side while she filled him in on what little she knew about the explosion.

Jeremy came awake slowly. The first thing he became aware of was how dark it was, as if someone had tied a thick, black cloth over his eyes. For several moments, he couldn't be sure that he was conscious. Then he decided that he was, and had awakened in the middle of the night in his bedroom. The drapes must have been drawn on his windows, because the glow of the full moon, which had flooded his room the night before, was now just a skinny sliver of silver, shining like a tiny flashlight through what seemed to be a small crack between the heavy curtains. He was very annoyed with the housekeeper for closing the drapes. He liked them open. How many times did he have to tell her to leave his things alone? His mother had never messed with his stuff.

Then he shifted, and something sharp stabbed his spine. He let out a small, startled gasp and shifted again. This time, his back pressed down against something cold and hard. It felt nothing like his king-sized waterbed. That was soft and rippling and warm, like the ocean in July. What he was lying on now felt nothing like the ocean.

I'm not in bed, Jeremy thought with clarity. I'm not even at home. Where *am* I?

His head hurt. When he lifted a hand, with great effort because the space was so narrow, and touched the back of his skull, his fingers came away sticky and wet. Jeremy was horrified. He was bleeding? Why?

Forcing himself to concentrate, he struggled to get his bearings. He was lying on his back. His chest ached. He could see nothing but the pie-shaped slice of moonlight shining through the narrow open space above his head. If he wasn't at home . . . if he wasn't in bed . . . what was going *on*?

Using his hands, he felt slowly, carefully, around him, which he could only do by squeezing his elbows into his chest. The motion hurt his chest. Everything he touched was as cold as marble, and solid, very solid. Like stone.

Whatever it was, he realized as he continued exploring, was close to him on all sides. *Too* close. It was everywhere. He seemed to be lying between two layers of it, like the filling in a sandwich. And all of it was only inches above his face, behind his head, on top of his body, and beneath him. He could barely move his legs and arms, they were pinned so tightly between the layers.

Jeremy's heart sank. His breath began to come very rapidly. He was completely encompassed in stone. As if . . . as if he'd been buried in it!

"Oh, god," he murmured anxiously as the reality of his predicament began to sink in, "what happened?"

Then he remembered the brilliant flash of light, and the thunderous roar in his ears. In the chem lab. An explosion? Tim Beech? There had been an explosion? Had the building collapsed?

"Oh, my god," Jeremy repeated, his heart pounding furiously, "am I *buried* here?"

Kate heard raised voices the minute she stepped from the elevator into Intensive Care. One of the voices was pleading, the other crying out in protest. She recognized the second voice as Margo's. Margo had used that same plaintive cry in math class, insisting to the teacher that she hadn't had time to do the homework because she'd had endless hours of gymnastics practice. "I just can't get it all *done!*" she had argued the Thursday before in calculus. She had sounded very close to tears then, just as she did now.

Margo *was* looking a little weird lately, Kate remembered, moving toward the source of the voices. When I saw her with Sam at the movies last Saturday night, I knew there was *something* not quite right about her. But I never once thought "eating disorder."

When she reached the doorway to the main ICU room, where a dozen beds were placed in neat, roomy cubicles separated by glass-windowed walls and containing every kind of life-support equipment, Kate hesitated. Only immediate family was allowed into the cubicles, although she had broken that rule more than once during the virus epidemic, visiting Damon Lawrence, a young fireman, because his mother couldn't come very often. And, of course, his father was nowhere to be seen.

There didn't seem to be anyone waiting to see Margo, either. Maybe the hospital hadn't been able to contact her parents yet. At any rate, it sounded like the nurse had her hands full.

"If you don't eat," the tall, heavyset nurse named Rosie Murphy told Margo in a firm voice while Kate listened from the hallway, "you won't get well. And if you don't get well, you'll be here with us for a very long time, hooked up to that nasty IV. You don't want that, do you?"

The only food Kate could see in the room was a shallow white bowl filled with what looked like clear broth. Not something *she* would call food. Pizza was food. Baked potatoes loaded with butter and cheese and bacon bits, *that* was food. But Kate knew that even if Margo were willing to try something as solid as pizza or a baked potato, her system might not be able to tolerate it by now. The girl had been cutting back too sharply on calories . . . maybe cutting them out entirely. Even if they could get her to chew and swallow, her body would reject the food. But not the broth. She should be able to keep that down, *if* they could get her to eat it.

Kate rapped lightly on the door. When Rosie glanced up, Kate signaled with a crook of her finger. The nurse came to the door and opened it. "What?" Her tone was impatient. Kate wondered how long the argument had been going on.

"I know her," she said, gesturing toward the bed. "Margo. Do you want me to give it a try? I only have a minute. But I might be able to help while I'm waiting."

"You're a friend of hers?" Nurse Murphy asked skeptically, toying with the stethoscope around her neck. She looked sorely tempted. The truth was, letting someone else take over briefly would give her the break she'd been craving for the past thirty minutes. She hadn't had lunch, and there were rumors about an explosion on campus. If the rumors were true, ICU could be getting some pretty heavy traffic before her shift ended. It might be now or never for her break.

"We're not really friends," Kate answered honestly. "But we go to the same school, she's dating my friend's brother, and we're the same age. She might listen to me. Besides, this isn't the first case of anorexia I've seen."

Rosie Murphy bristled. "No one said that's what she's got! Where did you hear that?"

Kate understood instantly. Margo Porter's parents were wealthy. They were prominent in community affairs and, according to Kate's mother, generous in their contributions to the medical complex. They wouldn't be at all happy if the word got out that their only child, their "perfect" daughter who had made them so proud by excelling in a sport, suffered from an eating disorder.

"My lips are sealed," Kate assured the nurse. "Do you want me to have a shot at it or not?"

Nurse Murphy gave in to temptation. "I wouldn't, except that I heard there was an explosion on campus."

Kate stared at her. "That's what the noise was? An explosion? On campus?" Susannah, Abby,

Jeremy, and Will were all over there. Sam was probably already there, too. People she cared about. People she cared about a *lot*. "Where?"

"I don't know. I'm not even sure it's true. But it sure *sounded* like an explosion. Anyway," the nurse went on, "I wouldn't mind grabbing a quick cup of coffee while you see if you can talk that girl into swallowing a couple of spoonfuls of clear liquid. But don't tell any of the other nurses I let you in here, okay? This girl's parents would have my head on a silver platter if they found out I'd handed her over to a volunteer."

When the nurse had scooted off to the lounge, Kate slipped inside the room and moved to the head of the bed. She was half listening for the wail of approaching ambulances even as she said hello to the patient. *Where* on campus had that explosion taken place?

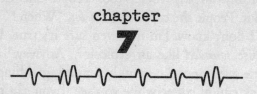

Margo looked up at Kate silently, with dull eyes. Her hair, once dark and silky, was dry and lackluster, thin and wispy as an infant's around her forehead and temples. Her skin, too, was dry and white, like tissue paper, all of the life drained out of it by a lack of essential vitamins. There was a trace of her former prettiness in the high cheekbones and perfectly shaped mouth, but only a trace.

She doesn't look the least bit like the kind of girl Sam Grant usually dates, Kate thought, feeling pity for the patient. How, she wondered angrily, could Margo have become this ill without anyone noticing?

"I know what you're thinking," Margo said, so quietly that Kate had to bend over the bed to hear her. "I can see it in your face. You think they should make me eat, don't you? You think it's just perfectly fine if they stick me with needles and feed me through tubes. But it's not. It's *wrong*! They don't have the right to do that to me. This is America. I have the right to decide what and when I should eat."

"They just want you to *live*, Margo," Kate said bluntly. "You're too thin. I don't get it. You're an athlete. You *know* you have to eat."

The eerily pale face turned weakly from side to side on the pillow. "Everyone keeps *saying* that. But I have eyes. I have mirrors in my house, and there are plenty of mirrors at the gym. If I so much as *look* at a cookie, I can see all those calories going straight to my hips." Margo's voice sank. "I *have* to stay thin for competition."

Kate knew better. She was sure it couldn't be gymnastics that kept Margo from eating, not really. There had to be something else, something that went a lot deeper than somersaults and tumbling. But she also knew it would do no good at all to say so. She wasn't qualified to give this girl the help she so desperately needed. "Don't your coaches think you're too thin?"

In an almost conspiratorial whisper, Margo answered, "They keep telling me I should eat, but I know why they're doing it. There's this new girl. Tracy Withersteen. She's only eleven. She's really tiny and skinny and she's better on the balance beam than I am. I know everyone wants her to replace me on the team. Because she's skinnier, and better. *That's* why they keep telling me to eat. So I'll get fat and have to quit the team and Tracy can take my place."

Kate didn't think *that* was true, either. But what mattered was that Margo believed it.

"I don't want to talk about me anymore," Margo said wearily. "What could be more boring? Hey, I heard there was an explosion on campus. Is that what that horrible noise was a little while ago? Where's Sam? He didn't go over there, did he? I need him here."

"I don't really know what happened. But, yes, Sam did go over there. He had to meet his parents. He'll be back. He asked me to keep an eye on you, and I said I would."

"Well, don't worry about it, because I'm not staying." Margo's lower lip came forward in a sullen, childish pout. "They can't keep me here against my will. That's the same thing as kidnapping, practically. I'm out of here as soon as I get my clothes back. Will you find out what they did with them? You can do that, can't you? I mean, you work here."

"Your leotard is ruined, remember? We had to cut it off you. Did you bring any other clothes with you?"

Margo groaned. "Oh, great! No, I didn't bring other clothes. I didn't exactly know what I was doing after I fell, you know what I mean? One of the coaches should have given my jeans and sweater to Sam or one of the paramedics. Now I'll have to call my mother and tell her to bring something. And she's so out of it these days, she'll never remember."

"I'll call her for you," Kate offered. She didn't feel that she'd done much, so far, to help Sam's friend. There didn't seem to be much she *could* do.

"No," Margo said hastily. "I can do it."

Kate noticed that her teeth were discolored. Impossible to believe that a gorgeous, popular, sought-after hunk like Sam Grant hadn't dumped this girl weeks ago. Maybe he felt sorry for her, but that didn't seem like the same Sam Kate knew.

"If you're not going to get me some clothes," Margo said dully, "just go away, okay?" She turned her face away from Kate.

"Tell you what," Kate said, picking up the spoon nesting in the bowl of broth. "I'll get out of your hair as soon as you take one little spoonful of broth, okay?" She tipped the spoon into the broth, filling it, and extended it toward Margo.

The girl's eyes widened in alarm. The look on her face as the spoon advanced toward her stopped Kate cold, halting the spoon in midjourney. It was a look of pure terror. Margo shouted, "No!" Her left hand flew up and, with astonishing strength for someone so frail-looking, slapped the spoon out of Kate's hand, sending it spiraling across the room.

Before a stunned Kate could figure out what to do or say, an ambulance shrieked, announcing its approach to the hospital. At the same moment, Rosie Murphy rushed back into the room. "Incoming, from the blast site. You're wanted downstairs. I'll take care of things here. Go. *Run!*"

Telling Margo she'd see her later, Kate ran.

When she arrived in trauma room C, a young man with badly singed dark hair and a nasty-looking laceration on his forehead was trying his best to tell Susannah and Will, two police officers, a fireman, and half a dozen staff members exactly what had taken place on campus. But he was dazed, disoriented, and in a great deal of pain from burns, lacerations, and a broken arm.

Although Kate was distracted by the sickening realization that something very serious had happened on campus, she was relieved to find three of the people she cared about standing in the center of the room, intact. One of those three, the fireman, was Damon Lawrence. Her heart jumped when she saw him. Kate hated it when that happened. She didn't want her heart to do *anything* when Damon Lawrence was around. But she didn't seem to have any control over it.

A nurse doused the young man's burns with sterile saline solution. An X-ray technician brought in a portable machine to take films of the broken arm and the patient's chest, although he hadn't complained of chest pains. An oxygen mask was kept over his face until the results of his blood gases returned from the lab. When they showed that oxygen was circulating properly in his blood, the oxygen mask was removed. Dr. Shumann began dressing the laceration on his head, and an Orthopedic man arrived to tend to the broken arm. Kate recognized him as the same doctor who had set Margo's arm.

Throughout all of this, the patient tried to give them information, but he kept drifting in and out of consciousness. As Dr. Shumann prepared to stitch up the nasty forehead cut, the medication began to take effect, and the patient's words began to slur.

Damon seemed particularly anxious for the injured young man to tell them — before the medication really kicked in — everything he could remember. "Can you tell us how many people we're talking about here?" he asked the patient, his words brittle with tension. "How many might have been in the building?"

Kate, standing at his side, admired the way he got right to the point. Damon hadn't been a fireman that long, but he certainly seemed to know what he was doing. Tall, thin, with eyes so dark, they sometimes seemed completely black, and thick, dark hair, Damon Lawrence had been in her life when they were both small, as a friend of hers and Will's. Then she'd lost of track of him after he dropped out of high school to work a dead-end job at the refinery.

But she'd learned when the viral epidemic took Damon as one of its victims that he had shaped up. He had actually gone back for his GED and become a fireman. That had surprised her.

She'd been even more surprised to discover that she was very attracted to him. It seemed to be mutual. Damon had this way of smiling at her that practically shouted, *This fireman won't settle for just being friends, Kate!* She kept fighting the attraction, because romance was definitely not on her schedule. She had college and medical school ahead of her, and none of it was going to be easy. She couldn't afford to let anything . . . or anyone . . . distract her.

Most of the time now, she felt like the wishbone on a holiday turkey, with her attraction to Damon tugging on one half of her, and her plans for a medical career tugging on the other half. She was almost certain that she couldn't tend to both and do a good job. *Almost* certain . . . but not quite.

"I don't know how many people were in the building," the patient murmured, grimacing in pain as he spoke. An IV solution dripped into his uninjured arm, and sterile dressings covered most of his burns. He had been very lucky. "I can't be sure how many people I saw in the building. Maybe there were some I *didn't* see." He turned his face away, and his eyes closed. The medication was working.

Damon shook his head at the thought of poring through all that stone rubble in a random search for victims. An accurate head count would have been a big help.

He stood up and took Kate's hand, leading her from the trauma room. "I've got to get back over there. You people here better stay sharp, because we could be bringing in some heavy-duty cases. Who knows what's buried in all that mess?"

Kate stopped in her tracks in the middle of the hallway. The Science building . . . what on earth was the matter with her? She hadn't thought . . . not until now. . . . Reaching out for Damon's hand, grabbing it, bringing him to a halt, she said, "Damon, your father. Doesn't he . . . didn't you say he got a job working on the maintenance crews on campus at night?"

Rowan Lawrence had abandoned his wife and two sons when Damon was very young. He had only returned to Grant two months ago, and was once again living in the family home in Eastridge. Damon hadn't welcomed him. But he had told Kate he was hoping to go to college, after all, now that they had another income in the family. "That is, if he doesn't cut and run again," he had added bitterly. Kate knew he hadn't forgiven his father, and found it hard to believe they could ever have a decent relationship. But if Rowan Lawrence's return meant that Damon could go to college, the father finally would have done something good for his son.

Damon stopped, turned around. She couldn't read the expression on his face. "Yeah, I did say that."

"He wouldn't have been working in the Science building, would he?"

Still no facial expression. Damn, he was hard to read! "Yes, ma'am," he said lightly, "I do believe that is exactly where Rowan Lawrence told me he'd be working on this very evening. He was to be mopping floors in the Science building, from nine tonight until midnight. That's what the man said."

Kate glanced at her watch. It was nine-forty. The explosion had taken place about thirty minutes ago. "Maybe he hadn't started working yet, when it happened."

"Oh, I wouldn't bet on it. I gotta hand it to the man, he's left the house early for work every night since he started. Turned over a new leaf, he says."

"Damon . . ."

"Forget it. Gotta go. I'll call you when I know anything useful." Damon clamped his helmet back on his head.

As he turned away, she added quietly, "It's awfully cold out there tonight. Could someone trapped in all that mess freeze to death?"

"We'll get 'em out before then," he answered confidently. "We might have a few cases of hypothermia, though. It's twenty-six degrees outside right now. But we'll get them out before they turn into Popsicles." He glanced quickly around the ER, saw no sign of Kate's mother, wrapped one arm around Kate's slender waist, and bent his head to give her a quick but heartfelt kiss. "I'll call you," he promised, and left.

She could have shouted after him, "Don't *do* that! Don't catch me off-guard like that!" But it wasn't as if she hadn't enjoyed the kiss.

Watching him stride on down the hall toward the exit, Kate decided that if anyone could get those people out of the debris, Damon Lawrence could. He'd saved more than one life during that awful refinery fire last year. She could only hope he'd be more careful in this new emergency than he'd been during the fire. A *hot dog*, one of the older fireman had called him. But after the fire, other people, including the local newspapers, had called Damon Lawrence a hero.

Kate had to admit that if you were looking for heroes some place other than in a movie or a book, Damon was a pretty good choice. *Hot dog* or not, he *was* brave. Damon Lawrence was going to *be* somebody.

Susannah and Will, talking quietly, emerged from the trauma room and joined Kate in the hallway.

"Damon's father might be in that building," she said. "He acts like he doesn't care one way or the other, but I know he does."

"Oh, man," Will said, his mouth set grimly. "I don't believe this! I was hoping having his old man back would knock that chip off Damon's shoulder. Get him to cool it some."

They stood silently in the hall for several seconds, until a sudden voice coming from the PA system startled all of them, pulling them out of their concern for Damon. It was Kate's mother's voice, speaking clearly and rapidly. She was announcing bad news.

"We have an explosion on campus," Astrid Thompson said crisply. "We have a two-story collapse of a building. Unknown number of victims trapped in the debris. All emergency personnel are requested to gather, stat, in the first-floor conference room to receive details and procedural instructions."

Stat was hospital terminology for, "Get your butt in gear, fast!"

The three turned and hurried off in the direction of the conference room.

chapter

8

~W~WWV~WV~V~WV~

When everyone, including Will and Susannah, had arrived in the long, narrow conference room on the first floor of Grant Memorial, Nurse Thompson addressed the group with a solemn expression on her face. "I've just received official word. Fire Captain O'Donnell has called in with a complete size-up of the situation on campus. Here's the deal. There's been an explosion in the Science building. Two floors have collapsed. Unknown number of victims. Possible danger of gas leaking. City crews are on the scene now to assess that risk. Also, further collapse of the building is possible. There was a fire, but it's out. Passersby were injured, possibly more than a dozen. We're trying to dig them out now. But it looks like that could be just the tip of the iceberg. It's the people who may have been *inside* the building that we're most concerned about."

"They don't have any idea how many possibles?" a nurse called out, meaning victims.

"Not yet. I'm going over there, with Dr. Izbecki and as many staff members as we can spare. By then, the Fire Captain may have a better idea of how many people are inside, and we can decide whether or not to set up a triage area on the scene. We'll stay in touch with the staff here to let them know what to expect. I need volunteers at both ends. Some to go with me, others to hold down the fort here."

Hands shot up into the air. One of them was Susannah's. She wanted to be on the site. She had never been involved in a multiple-casualty incident, and although she hated what had happened, she was anxious to get her first look at the triage process Astrid had mentioned. That meant, she knew, quickly deciding the degree of injury to each patient and which ones should be treated *first*. They hadn't studied large-scale emergencies in their classes.

Besides, Will would be on site. He was a paramedic and could do more good at the blast site than in the hospital. She liked watching Will work. He was calm, efficient, and had the kind of soothing voice that calmed even the most frightened victims. She had learned a lot from working with him.

She was glad, too, that Dr. Izbecki was going. She had worked many times with Jonah Izbecki, a tall man whose tone could be brusque, but whose manner with the patients was gentle and considerate. Susannah didn't envy him the task he would be facing at the site. Deciding so quickly which patients required immediate care and which patients must wait for treatment would be very difficult. It was cold over there, dark except for the moonlight, and probably chaotic. There would be a crowd, and probably news media as well. Not the best circumstances for rapid diagnoses.

When every hand in the room flew up, Astrid said, "Those who want to go along, move to the right side of the room. If you're willing to stay here, an equally important job, instead of traveling to the front lines, stand against the left wall, please."

The room seemed to divide up fairly equally, which made Astrid's task easier. Susannah was surprised to see Kate on the left side of the room. That didn't seem like her, willing to stay behind instead of being right in the middle of things.

"I promised your brother I'd keep an eye on a friend of his," Kate explained a few minutes later as everyone hurried from the room. "Margo Porter. She's in ICU. Anyway, people are going to be needed here, too, when they start bringing survivors in."

"Margo? What's wrong with her?" Susannah didn't know the girl well. Because Grant High had an excellent gymnastics team and the private day school Susannah attended had none, Margo had opted for Grant. And Sam didn't make a habit of bringing his girlfriends to Linden Hall.

But Susannah had run into the couple a few times, at movies or dances. She remembered now, thinking that although Margo had a pale prettiness about her, she had looked very tired. She hadn't seemed like Sam's type. "If she's in ICU, she must be pretty sick."

Kate hesitated. Rosie Murphy had made it clear that any diagnosis in this case was to remain confidential. "I'm not really sure what's wrong with her, exactly. She *is* really sick, and Sam asked me to check on her once in a while. But when they start bringing survivors in, I might not have time. Listen," Kate added as they arrived in the ER lobby, "do me a favor, okay? You're going to be over there. Could you keep an eye out for Damon? If he starts to do something really stupid, tell him if he gets killed I'll never speak to him again."

From everything that Kate had said in the past about Damon, Susannah was pretty sure anything *she* said to him would fall on deaf ears. But she promised to try.

Kate stood in the doorway watching them leave, a wistful look on her face.

When the medical crew from Med Center arrived at the site of the blast, a well-organized command post was being set up by the first ambulance crews to arrive on the scene.

A tall, thin medic with a graying mustache approached Dr. Izbecki and Astrid to say, "Still no estimate of victims inside. We've dug a few out of the rubble outside and will be sending them to your ER any minute now. They were only passing by the building when the blast hit."

"How bad?" Astrid asked.

"I don't know. They were hit by flying stone, most of them, and some of them were buried under it. As for the building itself, it's anybody's guess how many were in there. It was after hours, so there's no way to estimate the number of people who might have been in a classroom or lab, or the science library. There were probably maintenance people in there, too. I'd say go ahead and set up a triage area. If we don't need it, fine, but it's better to be prepared, wouldn't you say? Did you bring tags? I don't have any."

Astrid nodded and held up a brown, letter-sized envelope, from which she extracted heavy paper triangles colored red or blue, green or yellow, with string handles.

Susannah, standing close to Will, whispered. "What are those for?"

"When they start bringing the injured out," he answered quietly, "if there are more than a few at one time, the staff will divide them into four categories. The tags identify the category. A red tag means a life-threatening injury that requires immediate intervention, like a clogged airway or isolated bleeding — something that has to be tended to right away."

Susannah watched Astrid passing the vividly colored tags around to staff members. "And the yellow tags?"

"Yellow is for victims with significant injuries, such as broken bones, that need treatment but aren't life threatening. The green is for the walking wounded, patients with minimal injuries who are okay on their own for the moment. Don't ask me why we use those particular colors for those particular categories. We just do. Everybody does it differently."

He had mentioned only three categories of injured. But Astrid was hanging out *four* separate sets of tags.

Already guessing the answer, Susannah asked, "And the blue?"

He let out an exasperated sigh. "They're for the dead and dying. People beyond help, or who need so much help that we'd be taking time away from people we *can* help. But we won't be needing the blue tags, Susannah. Anyway, it's possible we'll be bringing survivors out one at a time, which means we'll have time to give each patient all the care they need and won't have to tag any of them. The triage area is just a precaution, that's all."

Telling her to be careful, Will left to begin helping in the rescue efforts.

Susannah glanced around her. Down on the avenue, vehicles from radio and television stations and local newspapers were parked in the middle of the street, surrounded by a crowd that continued to increase in size.

On the next level, which was the slope below the building, the medical staff was busily setting up cots and medical equipment, with Nurse Thompson and Dr. Izbecki directing the operation.

And then, directly beyond that activity, there was the building itself. The lower two floors had melded into one another, and there were gaping holes in the upper floors where there once had been windows. Rubble seemed to be everywhere . . . littering the lawn outside, piled high inside like landfill.

Where, she wondered again, was Jeremy? Was he somewhere in all that mess? Had he still been in the building when its walls and floors and ceilings shook and then collapsed?

Susannah wanted desperately to be as optimistic as Abby. But she knew that if Jeremy *could* be on campus, finding out what had happened, he *would* have been.

And he wasn't. Jeremy Barlow was nowhere to be seen.

Riding upstairs in the empty elevator cage, it struck Kate that the hospital seemed eerily quiet, as if it were . . . waiting. Which, she reminded herself as she got off at ICU, it was. But in the meantime, there were other patients in the hospital, like Margo, who shouldn't be ignored.

As she passed the nurses' station, Kate asked Rosie Murphy, "Anybody in there with Margo?"

"Nope. Her parents were here. They were not at *all* happy. Dr. Kwan took them into her office to confer with them." She stuck a pencil behind one ear, under graying hair, and shrugged. "I suppose there's no reason why you shouldn't go in. Maybe you can do her some good. Just for a minute, though, Kate. Her folks will be back soon. Not that Margo seemed all that glad to see them. There's something going on there, if you ask me."

Nodding, Kate moved on down the hall, wondering exactly which aspect of Margo's illness her parents were so unhappy about. Was it the fact that their daughter had been hospitalized? Or the fact that she'd been hospitalized for an eating disorder instead of a nice, normal appendectomy or a bad case of the flu? Maybe what they'd tell all their friends was, Margo had fallen on the balance beam and broken an arm, and neglect to mention the fact that their daughter weighed only eighty-four pounds.

You're judging again, Kate, a stern, inner voice scolded. When are you going to quit doing that? You've never even met Mr. and Mrs. Porter. They could be very sweet, very concerned people who only want what's best for their child. At least wait until you've met them before you label them.

She opened the door to Margo's cubicle and stepped inside, saying, "It's quiet downstairs, so I . . ."

The room was empty.

In his cold, dark, stone cave, Jeremy heard sounds. At first he thought he'd imagined them, because he wanted so much to hear something, anything, that would tell him he was still a part of the real world. He had never felt so isolated, so abandoned, not even when his mother left. If she wanted to go, *let* her. If she didn't *want* to be there, who wanted her there? Not *him*.

Here, in this dark, frigid place, with only the tiny slice of moonlight to comfort him, it felt very much like how he imagined a coffin would feel, although he'd never been in one. He'd never even seen one.

The sounds came again. Voices. And this time, Jeremy was sure he hadn't imagined them. They seemed to be shouting. He couldn't hear them well enough to figure out just why they were shouting, couldn't distinguish if they were shouting in alarm or in a searching way or in anger. They were too far away. But at least they were *there*. Out there somewhere. Maybe they'd come this way and then he could shout, too, and someone would find him, get him out of this horrible stone crypt.

If only he could see. It was so frustrating, so frightening, to be lying completely hidden from view when it was likely that people were looking for him, but it was even worse not to be able to see what was going on. How much damage had the Science building suffered? What about Tim Beech? Was he still alive? Could he possibly still be alive when he had been sitting right smack in the middle of the explosion?

Probably not.

A sudden, intense pain in his skull brought Jeremy's head straight up in a reflex action. Too late, he realized that was a mistake. There was no room in his narrow trap for any kind of movement. The top of his head smacked into the top layer of stone. He struggled valiantly to stay conscious, aware even as his brain reeled that if he fell silent, his chances of being rescued diminished greatly, perhaps even disappeared completely.

But his head had already been aching, and he

was running short of air in his little cavern. Sighing in defeat, Jeremy slid into unconsciousness, wondering as he did so if anyone in the coffee bar would remember that he had been on his way to this building when he left there. If they did remember, maybe they would send someone to look. . . .

Kate stood in the entryway of Margo's ICU cubicle, uncertain about what to do. The bed, a tangle of white sheets, was empty. More telling, an IV needle, two slices of adhesive tape stuck to its tubing like fresh sticks of gum, swung freely beside the bed, a shiny pendulum telling Kate that Margo hadn't been gone long. If she had, the needle ripped from her arm would no longer be swinging. It would be dangling in place, motionless.

Knowing it was futile, Kate nevertheless searched, very quickly, every corner of the room. It wasn't a tiny space, but there was no place to hide. Because ICU patients were never ambulatory, there was no bathroom where Margo might be hiding, no shower, no closet. Kate's head swiveled from side to side, her eyes checking out the flanking cubicles through the glass windows. Both cubicles, both beds, were empty.

"Margo?" Kate's voice echoed hollowly.

There was no answer. Kate hadn't really expected one.

Turning on her heel, she ran to the nurses' station. "She's not in there. Could someone have taken her downstairs for tests?"

"What do you mean she's not in there? She's not scheduled for any tests." Nurse Murphy reached for the telephone at her elbow. "The girl has split," she said as she dialed security. "This is my fault. Her parents had an argument in her room and left angry, and Margo was very upset. I knew she was a flight risk. I should have kept a closer eye on her. There'll be hell to pay now." Sighing heavily, she began speaking into the phone.

Kate wasn't willing to wait for the officers. She ran for the door to the fire stairs. Margo couldn't have left by the elevator. To do that, she would have had to pass the nurses' station, and she would have been seen.

The metal door was heavy. Kate found it hard to believe the weakened girl could have found the strength to push it open. Even then, she would have had to take the stairs slowly. She was too weak to rush.

I'm faster than she is, Kate told herself, and descended the stairs two at a time, her sneakers making a soft, slapping sound on the bare concrete steps. She didn't call out Margo's name, afraid she'd scare her and spur the girl to run faster.

She found the patient halfway down, crumpled into a small, white ball on the landing between the second and third floors. Tiny beads of red gathered in the crook of her elbow where she had yanked the IV free. Her skin was so white, it looked lavender in the pale fluorescent lighting. She was conscious, her eyes open, tears of frustration pooling at the corners.

Kate stooped to feel for a pulse. It was there. But it was dangerously weak and thready, and when Kate leaned closer to listen to chest sounds, she didn't like what she heard. Margo's heart was beating far too rapidly.

"You almost made it to the first floor," Kate said, removing her smock to fold it and push it beneath the girl's head. "What on *earth* did you think you were doing? Don't you think someone would have noticed a skinny kid wandering around the hospital in nothing but this dinky little johnny?"

The answer came in a painful whisper. "I want *out* of here. I *told* you I was going to leave."

"You said you'd leave when you got your clothes. Doesn't look to me like that happened. Anyway, you can't leave. You're not well enough. And you won't be until you decide to eat real food again."

Margo held up the arm encased in white plaster of paris. "Don't say that!"

Exasperated, Kate cried out, "Look, we've got a crisis on our hands tonight. How about if you wait until tomorrow to pull this stuff, okay?" She bent to fasten one arm around the girl's stick-thin waist, at the same time trying to loop around her own shoulders Margo's good arm. It fell uselessly back down, as if it were made of straw.

"*Help* me here!" Kate begged. "You're heavier than you look."

Margo laughed giddily. "That's what I've been trying to *tell* everyone!" But she took a deep, raspy breath and threw her arm back up around Kate's shoulders.

When they emerged from the stairwell into a first-floor corridor full of orderlies, nurses, volunteers in pink uniforms, and visitors in street clothing, everyone stopped what they were doing to stare. They seemed paralyzed by the sight of a tall, slender girl with dark, cornrowed hair, her mouth tense from the strain of supporting the thin figure staggering along beside her.

She's going to pass out any second now, Kate thought with certainty, and snapped loudly, "Well, don't just stand there staring, people! Get me a gurney and an IV setup and a nurse to check this girl's vitals. We need to get her back upstairs to ICU."

Dr. Lincoln, a tall, attractive woman in her thirties who was a favorite of Kate's, strode over to take the fainting girl from Kate's arms. "What on earth . . . ? How did she get down here?"

"She *walked*," Kate answered, rubbing her shoulder. "The girl took a hike. Came down the fire stairs. It seems," she added as the doctor listened to Margo's lungs, "that she's not happy with our accommodations."

"Sorry to hear that," Dr. Lincoln murmured, gesturing to an orderly to deposit the patient on a gurney. "We may have to put her in restraints."

Kate swallowed hard. Restraints? Margo might have to be strapped into her bed? A revolting idea. "Isn't that against the law or something?" She knew it wasn't, not if the measure was necessary for proper medical treatment, but privately, she thought it *should* be illegal. Margo wasn't a prisoner, after all.

Sam had asked her to look out for Margo. Feeling a sudden, strong urge to defend the girl, Kate said, "Maybe she's upset about the explosion on campus. The boy she's dating went over there, and Margo's probably worried about how he is."

Dr. Lincoln lifted her head and gazed at Kate through her glasses. She slipped Kate's *dashiki* out from under the patient and handed it to Kate. "So she was going to go over there in her little johnny-coat in twenty-degree weather? I wouldn't consider that a rational idea, would you, Thompson?"

Kate had no answer for that.

With Margo prone on the gurney, covered with a sheet, the doctor inserted a new IV needle. "She's dehydrated. Dangerously so. I'll see that she gets back upstairs. You'd better get back to Emergency. They could be bringing people in from the blast site any second now."

"Is she going to be all right?" Kate asked, thinking of Sam. No wonder **he'd** asked Kate to keep an eye on Margo. He must have known she needed supervision.

Dr. Lincoln shook her head. "Beats me. Her electrolytes are probably way out of whack, and I don't like the way her heart sounds, either. I think I'll have Dr. Barlow take a look at her."

Margo heard the name and said, "I don't need a heart specialist. I just need to get out of here."

"Right." Dr. Lincoln signaled to the orderly to take the patient back to ICU.

When she had gone, Kate, feeling tired and depressed, leaned against the wall, watching the activity around it, but not really seeing the volunteers and visitors and medical staff passing by her. She was thinking about Margo Porter. Until today, she had hardly known Margo. Now she was beginning to feel responsible for her.

That was stupid. It was *Sam* who was supposed to be concerned about the girl, not Kate Thompson. He had a lot of nerve, Sam did, expecting *her* to check on his girlfriend. If he was so worried, why didn't he stay at the hospital instead of taking off for the blast site?

On the site, rescue efforts began in earnest. The medical staff divided itself in half. The first group began treating the passersby who had been unearthed, while the second group, moving to a safe distance from the building in case of further explosions or collapse, established a triage area. Cots had been set up and were quickly occupied by shaken patients with varying degrees of injury. Thick piles of blankets brought from Med Center were stacked on more tables, beside medical equipment. Although the moon continued to bathe the scene in a bright silver glow, a dozen portable lights and an accompanying generator were brought in by the fire department to provide better lighting for the rescue work.

Firemen and paramedics, and volunteers — that included Sam and a group of his friends — armed with flashlights or lanterns, had already begun moving into the debris.

Susannah knew the task of finding survivors inside the wreckage wasn't going to be easy. Searching hands would get numb from the cold, footing would be treacherous, and the workers would be fighting the fear of further structural collapse.

"Here's what we think happened," the Fire Captain told them when he'd finished his initial assessment of the damage. "It looks like the explosion took place on the second floor, and it sent that floor crashing down upon the first. That floor is still holding, hasn't sunk into the basement, although it could at any time. The blast also cut a huge hole in the third floor. What's left of that floor is holding, too. But it's pretty shaky. If it goes, and crashes straight down to the first floor, the added weight will be too much and all of it will collapse into the basement. So we need to get any survivors out of there as quickly as possible. One good thing, the city crew says there's no longer any danger of a gas leak." He glanced around the triage area. "You all set here?"

Dr. Izbecki, his face red with cold, nodded even as he hastily splinted the broken arm of a young man who had been jogging past the building when the explosion took place. "Do you have any better assessment of how many victims we might be talking about?"

The commander shook his head. "Unfortunately, no. Could be six, could be sixty. We've got volunteers down there in the crowd," he said, pointing toward the avenue, "asking questions, trying to get a more accurate head count. Finding out who has a friend or relative missing, who doesn't, that kind of thing. Too bad this building didn't have a sign-in sheet, like some of the dorms and frat and sorority houses. If it did, and if we could find it in all this mess, we'd know exactly who'd gone into the building and hadn't come out when the blast hit."

When he turned and hurried back to the site, no one on the medical staff said anything. Instead, they busied themselves wrapping the bloodied survivors in warm blankets and seeing to their wounds. "Warm any IV solution before you hook it up," Dr. Izbecki cautioned. "These people may be bordering on hypothermia. Cold fluid internally would drop their core temperature further. Put the packets inside your coats and use your body heat to warm them if you have to."

Susannah, pouring hot coffee from a trio of thermoses, counted heads. Six cots, all occupied, with three people sitting up, three more unable to. Six patients headed for the ER at the same time. Was there enough staff left behind to handle the load?

Earlier, the scene up on the slope had looked so chaotic from where Susannah had been standing that she had dreaded moving into its midst. She was relieved to find that in spite of the sense of urgency, there *was* a system in place, and the medical staff seemed to be in control.

When all six patients had been loaded into ambulances, Susannah glanced around, looking for Callie. Callie might know if Jeremy actually had been inside the building.

It took her several moments to locate the girl in bright red. She was standing between Abby and Sid Costello, Abby's boyfriend and a patient at Rehab, seated in his wheelchair. A near-fatal fall from the top of a water tower the previous summer had placed the former athlete in the chair. In the past several months, he had made significant progress, and Abby was optimistic now that Sid would walk again.

But then, Susannah reminded herself as she hurried to join them, Abby was optimistic about practically everything. That was part of her charm. Abby did a lot of volunteer work at Rehab, where she had met Sid. It was unquestionably her upbeat personality and no-nonsense attitude that had pulled Sid back from the pit of despair and stirred him to fight again, just as he had on the football field.

But it wasn't gratitude that Susannah saw in Sid's dark brown eyes when he looked at Abby. It was something very different. And Abby had a matching look in her eyes. They sparred a lot, back and forth, but Susannah sensed the deep affection between them, and she envied them. Abby and Sid were so comfortable with their feelings for each other, while she and Will struggled so with theirs.

Susannah made her way through the cots and waiting gurneys to the trio standing next to a portable table. Abby and Sid were staring silently at the devastation. Just as Susannah arrived, she heard Callie say in her thin, high voice. "Well, what's the point, Sid? It's not like you can help. And that chair of yours is just going to get in the way."

If the cruel remark had come from anyone else, Susannah would have been shocked. But it was typical of Callie. Susannah had made excuses for her for a while, because she knew Callie's mother was chronically ill, and she admired the fact that with Callie's father so busy, it was Callie who regularly brought Mrs. Matthews to Emsee for her dialysis treatments. But Susannah had reached the point where she was ready to admit that Callie was a lousy friend. Not even a very good acquaintance, for that matter.

She had to give Sid credit. He, too, must have considered the source of the remark, because he didn't wince at Callie's words. And before Abby could jump in and defend him, which Susannah knew she was about to do, judging by the narrowing of her thickly lashed eyes, Sid countered lightly, "Jealous, Callie? Because you have to walk while I get to ride?"

Callie laughed, a brittle sound. "I ride. I have a brand-new car, remember?"

"Yeah, but I don't have to buy gas," Sid said, smiling up at a fuming Abby to reassure her that Callie wasn't getting to him.

Before Abby could explode, Susannah asked, "Have any of you seen Jeremy?"

Callie stared at her. "Susannah, what's the matter with you?" she asked rudely. "You were in the coffee bar earlier. You know as well as I do" — she pointed a red-gloved finger in the direction of the ruined building — "that Jeremy is in *there*!"

chapter
10

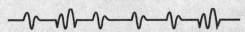

Jeremy knew he was fading in and out of consciousness, because every once in a while, the sliver of moonlight and the unyielding sharp edges of stone would fade away. And then there was nothing. He wasn't aware of his eyes opening and closing, but he knew they must have, because suddenly, there would be the silver ribbon of light again and there would be the slabs of stone entrapping him.

Each time it happened, he had no way of knowing how long he had been out. But nothing had changed. Nothing at all. The rubble hiding him from sight hadn't been lifted off him, his head hadn't stopped hurting, and there were still sounds out there somewhere, dull and distant, but there.

He thought that was a good sign, that it hadn't suddenly gone completely quiet. Didn't that mean there were people out there moving chunks and slabs of stone, searching for him? Didn't that mean he wasn't alone, after all?

He tried to clear his throat, tried to shout. But

he had been buried for some time now with nothing at all to drink. His mouth and throat felt like he'd been eating sand. When he opened his lips, no sound slipped out. He tried again, and again, but never managed anything above a whisper.

How could they find him if he couldn't tell them where he was?

When the ambulances carrying the six passersby screeched to a halt at Med Center's ER, the first survivor unloaded was in serious distress. Kate, an attending physician, a nurse, and four orderlies stood shivering under the canopy. They had already been alerted by ambulance radio that time was crucial for this patient.

"This one's got a head injury," the first paramedic to leave the vehicle announced. "Right pupil distended, pulse sixty, breathing shallow but regular. Dr. Izbecki said to watch for increased intercranial pressure. It looks like he was right. We've hyperventilated with one hundred percent oxygen, and positioned the head to reduce any venous pooling, but he's still in distress."

"What's the body weight?" Dr. Shumann asked as they ran with the gurney to a trauma room. Other gurneys, with the remaining patients, were right behind them, but Kate realized, glancing quickly behind her, that none were as critical as this patient.

"One eighty-five, according to his driver's license. Name's Lars Pedersen."

In the trauma room, the doctor ordered a drug Kate knew was commonly used to control swelling in the skull from head injury. It wasn't used by paramedics en route to the hospital because they had no way of knowing what was going on in the brain, and using the drug incorrectly could result in further damage.

"Get blood gases and a CAT scan," the doctor ordered, "while I call Dr. Jacobs in Neurosurgery. I want him to take a look at this boy."

Kate was given the vials of blood to rush to the lab. As she ran down the hall, she was conscious of the bustling activity in treatment rooms on both sides of her: an eye being bandaged in one, a cast being applied to an ankle in another, bloody faces, bloodied limbs, people crying quietly or asking in tremulous voices if they were *really* going to be okay. And there were still emergencies that weren't connected to the blast. Two young boys had been fighting over the last Pop-Tart in the box. The smaller boy had thrust a kitchen fork into the toaster to retrieve the treasure and had been knocked flat by the electrical charge. A resident was lecturing both boys on the dangers of electricity.

There was a cardiac case in trauma room D being worked on by Dr. Barlow, and a bad case of the flu in treatment room four.

Kate's feet flew. We should have kept more staff here, she thought as she ran. How are we going to handle all of this?

When she returned to Lars Pedersen's trauma room, clear liquid, similar to IV fluid, was dripping from the patient's right ear.

She heard Dr. Shumann, standing at the house phone, say clearly, "My guess is, basilar skull fracture with an epidural hematoma. I'm sending him up to you for a CAT scan. I'd say the rest is up to you. Good luck." She hung up, a grim expression on her face.

Fractured skull, Kate told herself. Bleeding in the brain, and maybe a blood clot, which could be fatal.

One of the patient's arms, the one with an IV needle, lifted suddenly and waved toward the ceiling, as if it were saying good-bye to a friend. Then it fell.

"Get him upstairs," the doctor said flatly. "Jacobs is expecting him. This kid had better be on an operating table before fifteen minutes are up."

Tubed and wired and IV'd, the patient, eyelids fluttering, was rushed from the room.

When he had gone, a dismal silence fell. "Well," Dr. Shumann said with false heartiness, "I guess there's no point in making Jacobs the bearer of bad tidings, is there? I'll call the parents." She pointed to the chart in Kate's hands. "You have a phone number there?"

Kate nodded and handed her the chart, saying, "His parents live in Vermont."

When she, too, had left the room, a nurse stripped the table of its paper linens and wadded them up into a ball. "This, my friends," she said, "was only the first of many, if I'm not mistaken."

While Susannah went to look for Will to find out how rescue efforts were going, Abby went over the "call sheet" requirements with Astrid. Because Abby seldom volunteered in ER, she wasn't familiar with the emergency routine.

The call sheets were used by paramedics to gather information on each patient. Astrid had decided it made more sense for volunteers to fulfill this important task since the paramedics would have their hands full without the added burden of extracting information.

If the patient was unconscious and unable to answer simple questions such as name and address and medical history, Abby was told to skip that part and go straight to the nature of the injury, also to the vital statistics such as blood pressure, pulse, respirations, state of consciousness, as they were dictated to her. Identification would have to wait, especially for those patients taken to the red area.

"All of the survivors will probably have identification on them somewhere," Astrid told Abby, "but locating it is not your job. Leave that to the police. For preliminary identification, use a number at the top of the call sheet and write that same number on the triage tag of each patient."

Sid offered to help. Abby knew Sid was frustrated because Sam and Will and Damon were all helping with rescue efforts, and Sid couldn't. Thanks to a vigorous exercise regime at Rehab, Sid had incredible upper body strength, and could have been a big help in lifting debris off victims . . . if he could *get* to the site. But he couldn't. Negotiating a wheelchair over those piles and lumps and bumps of broken stone would be impossible.

Her heart ached for him. He made such a point of sitting up straight in his chair, always, to look taller and more in command. He seldom complained, although occasionally he still fell into one of his old rages, usually when some facility in Grant wasn't equipped for wheelchairs. And although he had little patience with adults who stared at him, he was very sweet and kind to children who asked him directly, as children tend to do, why his legs didn't work.

He wanted to be of some use now, but it only took one person to fill out call sheets.

Saying he'd see her later, Sid wheeled himself

away from Abby, and headed toward the site.

Abby restrained herself from calling after him, "Be careful!" He hated it when she said stuff like that. "I already *have* a mother," he would retort sharply.

Taking a deep breath, Abby glanced around her. Nurses were cleaning up after the first group of survivors, rescue workers taking a brief break were sipping hot coffee to take the chill out of their bones, Dr. Izbecki and Nurse Thompson were conferring quietly in the red area. And ahead of all of that activity lay the damaged building, bright with moonlight and the yellow beams of the portable lights. She still couldn't believe it had happened, couldn't shake the feeling that what she was looking at was just a scene from a movie.

But those people who only had been passing by the building, those first survivors with their bloodied faces, their eyes dulled with shock and the same kind of disbelief that Abby was feeling, they'd been real enough, hadn't they?

Sam and five of his friends, along with other rescue workers, including Will and Damon, moved cautiously through the blast site, removing debris.

In the triage area, Abby and Susannah doublechecked supplies, filling any gaps where they found them. They made Callie help, in spite of her protests that "the sight of blood makes me hyperventilate!"

"The most common injuries in this type of incident," Astrid told all three girls, "will be lacerations, some of which will be serious and require stitches, even surgery, in some cases. Those patients who need stitches will have to be transported by ambulance to Med Center. The shallower cuts must be disinfected, perhaps dressed. We *can* do that here. If the cut is on or near the head, the patient will be dispatched by ambulance for a CAT scan of the brain. We may have concussions and other head injuries, including skull fractures. Those patients, too, will be sent to Emsee. Just do the best you can to keep up with what the staff needs."

While they waited for more survivors to be uncovered, tension in the triage area built to an almost unbearable level. Susannah spilled every cup of coffee that she poured because her hands were shaking with cold, and with anxiety about Jeremy, and about Will and her brother, both of whom were working on the site. Callie, who was supposed to be helping, seemed to be doing nothing but whining about how cold it was. The sound of her high, nasal voice complaining was like chalk on a blackboard to Susannah.

She finally snapped. She whirled on Callie, crying, "*Will* you shut up? Everyone already knows it's cold, Callie. You don't need to keep reminding us. Why don't you find something useful to do? Double-check supplies or something. Maybe that will warm you up."

Callie pouted. "I don't work at Emsee. I don't know anything about supplies. I only stayed here because Sam is here. Anyway, we already double-checked everything."

"Then *triple*-check it. Just get out of my hair."

Susannah had just put Callie to work counting boxes of gauze rolls when there was a shout from the crowd down on the avenue. Dreading the worst — had the third floor collapsed? — Susannah's head jerked up.

Two firemen, one of whom she recognized as Kate's friend Damon, were bringing out another victim from the building. Will and his partner were right behind them. They scooped a waiting stretcher off the ground and held it aloft for the patient. Susannah could tell by the gentle way the firemen lifted the young man that he was injured. Some people might be rescued unharmed from the site, but not this first one.

Susannah ran to help.

11

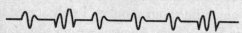

"**M**ale, early twenties," Will said calmly as he and his partner arrived at the red area with the stretcher. "Conscious, but disoriented. No knowledge of what happened. Laceration on right parietal area. Right femur broken. Possible head trauma."

Susannah saw a large, bloody cut on the right side of the patient's chest. Whatever had landed on him had gouged right through his navy blue wool jacket. There was another deep cut at his right temple, and his jeans were ripped open over his broken thigh. He was barely conscious, his eyelids fluttering in distress.

When the patient had been transferred to one of the waiting cots, Dr. Izbecki and Nurse Thompson took over, moving swiftly and efficiently. "Pupils equal and reactive," the doctor announced as a nurse began an IV, using a packet she had been keeping warm inside her jacket. "Abdomen soft, breath sounds bilaterally clear. Ecchymosis around both eyes, multiple abrasions to face, left shoulder, and both arms. We need a traction splint, sandbags, cervical collar, and a backboard. Get a monitor on this guy, stat!"

Susannah understood most of the language. *Ecchymosis* was a medical term for bruising. A bruise under each eye, such as this patient had, was commonly called *owl eyes*. It meant that the skull had taken quite a blow, and could be fractured.

When the patient had been hooked up to a portable cardiac monitor, Astrid called out, "Pulse one hundred. Respirations are twenty, and blood pressure is one twenty-four over eighty. Monitor shows a sinus rhythm."

The man, who looked to be a university student, had been lucky. The sinus rhythm meant that although his skull might be injured, his heart was functioning okay in spite of the chest injury. So far, anyway.

The thigh was quickly splinted, the young man's spine immobilized, and he was carefully lifted to a gurney with a backboard.

"Oxygen by cannula at six-one," the doctor ordered the paramedics preparing to transport the patient to a waiting ambulance. "Keep an eye on his breathing. If his pulse drops, give him one hundred percent oxygen and call me on the radio. Even if it doesn't, call me when you get to

Med Center, let me know how he handled the trip."

As the haunting sound of the siren faded, Susannah asked Astrid, "Will he make it? That patient?"

The nurse nodded. "Probably. It's the head wound that's the most serious, I think. Like the last patient. Unless I miss my guess, the first thing they'll do when he gets to Emsee is an emergency craniotomy. Open up his skull and take a look at the damage. Then they'll fix him up, if they can. He must have taken quite a blow to the head." Astrid looked Susannah in the eye with a calm, direct gaze. "The night is just beginning, Grant."

Susannah let out a deep sigh. She knew Astrid was probably right. But she couldn't help wishing that just this one time, just this once, Kate's mother was wrong.

When the Fire Captain returned to the triage area for a warming cup of coffee, he said tautly, "The way those two floors are sandwiched together leaves us very little room to work. I've sent men up to the third floor to shore up what's left of it, keep it from caving in on top of us, but that's not going to be easy. And they're risking their necks."

"You've got to get survivors to us faster than this," Dr. Izbecki said. "The temperature is dropping. It can't be more than twenty degrees out here. The people trapped in that building are going to be suffering from hypothermia. That will complicate treatment of any injuries they might have."

The Fire Captain nodded as he sipped his coffee. "We're trying our best."

"Does anyone know what caused it yet?" Astrid asked him. Her eyes were on the rescue workers scrambling over broken rock, illuminated eerily by the pale beams of the portable lights.

"Far as we can tell, someone was combining chemicals in the science lab on the second floor. The *wrong* chemicals. That's all we know so far. We'll get to the bottom of it, as soon as we have all the facts."

But, Abby thought, turning away, that won't help the people who were caught in the explosion. Including, probably, Jeremy. She was convinced now that he had never left the building. If he had, he'd have heard about the explosion by now and he'd be back on campus, wanting to help.

Abby hurried over to Callie, who, as far as Abby was concerned, had been of very little use so far. She was leaning against an ambulance in the staging area, nibbling on one of the cinnamon buns donated by a local bakery. They had just arrived, and were still warm. A flash of anger warmed Abby. Those buns were for the volunteer workers. How much work had Callie done?

"Callie, I want you to find a telephone and call Jeremy's house. Check with the housekeeper, see if he's there."

Callie plucked a plump, brown raisin from the bun and popped it into her mouth. She didn't move. "He's not home, Abby. You and I both know that." She flicked a hand behind her. "He's in there. Trapped. Maybe dead. A phone call would be a waste of time."

Abby fixed a steely gaze on the girl. Callie Matthews wasn't exactly swamped with close friends. Callie's closest friend, Tina Montgomery, had died in last year's viral epidemic. But Callie still had Jeremy. Jeremy was totally nonjudgmental, maybe because he thought people were always judging him and deciding he didn't measure up. He was one of the few who had stood by Callie all through high school, in spite of her temper tantrums, her mean spirit, and her selfishness. Now, here she stood, munching on a cinnamon bun and refusing to make a simple phone call to find out if her only real friend was safe.

Abby reached out and snatched the half-eaten bun from Callie's hand. "Callie Matthews, if you don't, right this minute, go find a telephone and call Jeremy's house, I will personally see to it that Sam never speaks to you again. *Ever!* And I *can* do that, Callie. Just watch me!"

The occasions when Abby O'Connor lost her temper were rare. Callie's mouth dropped open and her eyes widened. "Abigail!"

"*Do* it! Now! Go!"

Callie went.

When she had gone, Abby's eyes searched the slope for some sign of Sid, whom she couldn't locate, and then Susannah. She found her friend standing near the site talking with Will. She was carrying a tray holding Styrofoam cups.

Abby decided to join them. Maybe they could tell her how the search was going.

She was on her way there when a chorus of shouts broke out just ahead of her. Breaking into a run, she arrived at Susannah's side to find her best friend standing with her hands covering her mouth, her eyes wide, staring down at an indentation in the ground.

Abby's eyes followed hers, and a sickened gasp escaped her.

There were nine people lying there. The huge pile of debris that had been covering them had been removed by a group of volunteers that included Will, Sam, Damon, and, Abby was shocked to discover, Sid. He was sitting in his chair, his face and hands white with dust from the rubble, looking as horrified as everyone else.

This wasn't the time to ask him how he'd maneuvered the chair across broken rock.

Someone shouted, "Medic! Over here!"

Will, breathing hard from the labor of lifting the massive stone slab, stared down at the victims. Two, he realized immediately, were beyond any kind of help. One was a young woman, another an older, African-American man. He knew they were dead.

Damon, standing beside Will, saw the man at the same moment as Will, and felt his breath catching in his throat. His father? Had he been snatched away again so soon?

Damon stiffened. So what if it is? he asked himself angrily. It's not like we can't do without him. We did before.

Nevertheless, he was unwilling to move closer to check. He left that to Will, who had met Rowan Lawrence recently when he came to the hospital to be treated for an allergy attack, and who was already at the lifeless man's side, feeling for a pulse. Will knew, too, that Damon's father worked nights on campus, and had overheard the young fireman calling out softly as they began searching through the rubble, "Rowan? Rowan, you in there somewhere?"

When Will found no pulse, he lifted his head to meet Susannah's eyes. She had hoped no one would be taken to the blue area. He had told her that wouldn't happen. Now, he shook his head, and heard her cry out softly.

"So, who you got down there?" Damon finally had to ask. "I can't see his face. Ain't somebody we know, is it?"

Will knew instantly what Damon was asking. Gently, very gently, he turned the man over in order to see his face. When he had done so, he lifted his head a second time, this time to call out to Damon, "No. Not someone we know."

Damon waved a hand, acknowledging Will's understanding. His father wasn't down there, wasn't dead. But that didn't mean he wasn't dead somewhere else. They couldn't know that yet, not until they'd searched through every single inch of this mess.

Damon didn't want to be grateful that his father was still alive. He didn't want to feel anything about it, one way or the other. So he told himself that he was relieved because now he could still go to college, maybe, if he could get in. That was the only reason he cared what happened to Rowan Lawrence.

He knew what Kate would say about that. She'd poke him gently in the arm and say, "Oh, yeah, right. You are such a *ba-ad* dude, Damon." Then she'd smile, in that way she had of looking like she knew everything there was to know.

Well, she didn't. She didn't know what it was like to have your daddy walk out the door one Tuesday morning in March and not come back for fifteen years. Didn't know what it was like to have him come back when you were full grown and didn't need a man around the house because you'd already learned how to be one yourself. Kate Thompson couldn't have a clue how something like that could bite at you.

He couldn't think about all that stuff now. Those people lyin' there, they needed help. He'd help take care of them. Then he'd go back to hunting for his runaway daddy.

Will spotted at least two broken legs — one a compound fracture — and several deep scalp lacerations that might or might not mean brain injuries. There was a young woman clutching her chest as if she were in terrible pain. Even from where he stood, several feet away, he could hear the shallowness of her breathing. Aside from those injuries, he was looking at more bloody lacerations than he had seen in even the most serious automobile accident. The grass around them was scarlet, and slick when you stepped on it.

Dr. Izbecki came up behind Will and said, "These people are going to need cervical collars, backboards, and sandbags, stat! Jackson, go get them. Take Grant with you."

Will and Sam turned and ran for the triage area. Will was careful not to look at Susannah as he passed her, but he knew how sickened she must be.

The blue area was *not* going to remain empty.

chapter
12

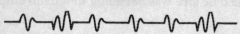

This time, when Kate went upstairs, she had two people to check on in ICU. Margo *and* Lars Pedersen, assuming his surgery was over. Sometimes neurosurgery took hours and hours.

"I'm sorry, Kate," Rosie Murphy informed her quietly. "Pedersen didn't make it."

Shocked, Kate leaned against the semicircular desk. "Didn't make it? He . . . he died?"

"About fifteen minutes ago. On the table. But Dr. Jacobs told me even if the kid had lived, he never would have been the same again."

Kate thought about that for a moment. Brain-damaged? Maybe his parents wouldn't have cared. Maybe they'd just be glad he was alive. She felt sick for them. They'd received the call from Dr. Shumann by now, were probably already on their way to Massachusetts from Vermont. Unless they had a car phone, they couldn't know their son hadn't survived the delicate surgery. They wouldn't know that until they arrived at Grant Memorial.

To erase the heavy feeling of sadness, Kate

tried to focus on the other reason she'd come to ICU. "Have you had any more trouble from Margo?"

"Nope. She's sleeping. Her parents went downstairs for coffee." Rosie shook her head. "They were hassling each other like a couple of cranky alligators. Each one blaming the other for the daughter's condition. Don't wake her up, okay? I have a feeling she doesn't get a lot of peace."

"Can I just take a peek? Maybe I'll leave her a note or something, tell her I was here."

The nurse handed Kate a pad and a pencil. "Make it quick. I'm not supposed to let you in here, you know."

"I'll just leave it on her tray table and she'll see it when she wakes up. It might cheer her up." After she had hastily scribbled the message, Kate strode down the hall to Margo's room.

To find it empty again.

Kate might have gone looking for the missing girl again if a disembodied voice hadn't declared, "All emergency personnel to ER, stat! Incoming from blast site. ETA one minute."

Kate turned and ran, calling out as she passed the nurses' station, "Margo's missing again! Better call security!"

Behind her as she reached the stairs, which were faster than the elevator, she heard, "Oh, no, not again!" But Kate kept going.

When she got downstairs, only one patient had arrived, but she knew the minute she rushed into the trauma room that he was in dire straits. Still conscious, he was extremely restless and confused. Tossing his head from side to side on the gurney, he repeatedly cried out, "It hurts, my chest hurts, *do* something, please!"

The room became a flurry of activity. Kate, her mind on Margo's disappearance, had to force herself to concentrate as Dr. Lincoln began snapping out orders. She called for portable chest X rays and spinal films, ordered blood to be typed and cross-matched, and asked for blood gases, which would reveal if the young man's oxygen intake and distribution were normal.

But they *can't* be, Kate thought with conviction; how could they be? Look at the way his chest is rising and falling. He's breathing as if giant pliers are squeezing his chest.

As the nurse at the young man's side called out vital statistics, Kate began writing them down on a chart. She didn't recognize the name, Joseph Kraft. A student, someone said, like Lars Pedersen. Kate hoped this patient would fare better than Lars had.

Dr. Lincoln, moving swiftly around the table, asked the nurse and an orderly to sit the patient partially upright so that she could listen to his chest. Kate wasn't happy about the expression on the doctor's face when that had been done and

Joseph Kraft, his face twisted with pain, was allowed to lie flat again.

"Cardiac tamponade," the doctor said flatly. "Get me a chest tray."

Kate ran for the tray. Joseph's heart actually *was* being squeezed, by blood collecting in the sac around it. A dangerous condition, one that would only worsen if it wasn't attended to immediately.

One nurse monitored the oxygen flow, another blood pressure, while still another handed Dr. Lincoln a syringe with a four-inch intracardiac needle. The skin of Joseph's rib cage was prepped, and the needle inserted near the seventh rib. There was no time for a proper anesthetic, and Kate was anticipating the patient's cry of pain. When it came, she wasn't surprised. But it chilled her, nevertheless.

When the needle had been advanced about three inches, the syringe suddenly began to fill with blood. Sickening as the sight was, Kate knew this was the blood that had been threatening to suck the very life out of this boy.

The first syringe was removed and a second inserted before Dr. Lincoln was satisfied.

Almost immediately, the boy's vital signs began to improve dramatically, and tension in the room eased.

"Well, well, well," the doctor said, smiling, "looks like this boy's a fighter. But he still needs a

CAT scan. I don't like the look of that wound on his head, and his thigh may need surgery. I would suggest someone remove this patient to the surgical floor and let the doctors up there decide who gets him first. After that, he'll be in ICU for a while."

Hearing "ICU," Kate remembered that Margo was missing. But before she could decide whether or not to go looking for her, there was another announcement, this one stating that two patients were on their way in from the blast site. According to the code, one would require the services of a plastic surgeon, whom Kate was assigned to locate.

Somebody else would just have to find Margo Porter.

Susannah tried to avoid looking at the blue triage area, where two black bags now lay side by side. A blue tag had been fastened to the zipper of each bag.

"Don't look over there," Will cautioned as he arrived in the yellow area with a man who had been walking his dog in front of the building when the explosion took place. The little dog was fine, unharmed and running around at the man's feet, whining to be picked up. "We've got our hands full with the other seven. I think Dr. Izbecki needs you."

Grateful to be busy, Susannah made her way through the cots to the doctor's side. He was busy examining a young man with a chest laceration, so Susannah moved to the two other patients sitting, dazed, on cots.

A girl with a deep cut over her left eye was terrified that she would lose the eye, there was so much blood pouring down her cheek. Susannah applied pressure to the wound with a gauze pad and assured the girl that the eye itself was intact, that the cut was closer to the brow, which it was. But the girl remained hysterical until one of the paramedics told her the same thing. Then she calmed down.

The woman sitting next to her, who said she was a teaching assistant, had a deep laceration on her left cheek. Susannah was sure it would require stitches, and might even leave a scar.

"Transport these two," Dr. Izbecki told Will, gesturing toward the two female patients. "One of them will need a plastic surgeon. I've already called ahead, he'll be waiting." He didn't say which one, but Susannah guessed it was the one with the cut on her cheek. She felt sorry for the woman. Every time she looked into a mirror from now on, she'd be reminded of this terrible night.

When that ambulance had pulled away, there were still five people being triaged. Abby moved quickly from one patient to the other, checking to see if she could get them anything, handing them sterile gauze pads to hold against their many cuts, assuring them that a doctor or paramedic would get to them quickly. Callie returned, saying no one had answered at Jeremy's house, and Abby recruited her, saying that if she wasn't willing to be useful, she would have to leave. "You can go stand in the crowd down on the avenue."

Callie didn't want to leave. So she stumbled around the triage area behind Abby. But after two minutes of looking at bloody faces, hands, heads, and chests, she made a noise low in her throat, covered her mouth with both hands, and fled the area.

Abby was able to move more quickly without Callie in tow.

A professor Abby had met once at Susannah's house was sitting on one of the cots, one hand over a bloody ear. She took him a cup of hot coffee, which he refused politely, saying his hands were too cold to hold it. "I don't think," he said as she put the cup back on her tray, "that I want to risk second-degree burns from spilled coffee. I believe that I have enough to contend with just now, wouldn't you agree?" Abby handed him instead a clean gauze pad to hold over the injured ear. He took it gratefully, and she saw as he applied the pad that the ear had been severed almost completely from his head. She wondered if that meant he had a head injury as well. He seemed lucid enough, but sometimes with a head injury you couldn't tell how severe the damage was until it was too late. She hoped that wasn't true of this man. He seemed very nice.

One ambulance after another wailed away from the blast site until the triage area, bloody and in disarray, was empty.

Abby and Susannah set about the task of restoring order. "For the next group," Astrid said, and both girls shuddered.

Damon Lawrence had moved into the building, stepping carefully through the layers of debris, his flashlight honed in on the area ahead of him. Navigating the stone rubble was hazardous. It was impossible to see if it was hiding a crevice in the rock beneath his feet, a treacherous split that a leg might slip into, becoming trapped. Then there was the fact that no one knew if the first floor was in danger of caving in, and the possibility of the rest of the third floor crashing down on top of rescue workers.

The rubble could be deceptive. Chunks of stone and wood could have fallen across a hole in the floor, covering it. Or the mess could be hiding a weak spot, one that needed only the weight of a human body to make it give way completely, sending the rubble, the flooring, *and* the human body crashing into the cold, dark depths of the building's basement.

He'd just have to take his chances. What choice did he have?

His father might be in here somewhere. Rowan. He couldn't call him "Father" or "Dad" or "Daddy." He couldn't say "Pop" or "Pa." His mother wanted him to, but he'd refused. A father was someone who was there while you were growing up. His hadn't been. So "Rowan" or "Hey, you" was the best Damon could do.

He was grateful for the portable floodlights. Still, he needed a flashlight to pick up the faintest sign of life in all this mess — a foot . . . a hand . . . a piece of clothing — jutting out from underneath the chunks and slices and slabs of stone and wood and blackboard. And he kept his ears alert to even the slightest sound . . . a murmur, a cry, no matter how feeble, maybe someone frantically scratching at the debris that kept him hidden from rescue workers. Listening was more difficult than looking, because there were other workers all around him, and although they were moving as cautiously as he was, as if they were walking through a minefield, it was impossible to move without sound.

Every time Damon's booted foot came down, he feared that it might be burying someone more deeply.

But when he finally did find his first survivor, she wasn't buried in rubble at all. She was intact, except for the fact that her left leg was firmly trapped between two huge slabs of concrete, rendering her immobile.

Damon knew the girl. Her name was Carmen Lopez, and she was from Eastridge. The place where she was half-lying, half-sitting, propped up on her elbows with nothing behind her to support her back, was in a dark corner untouched by the spotlights. Without the beam of his flashlight, he might have walked right by her.

"Carmen?" He made his way carefully toward her. A large chunk of rock teetered beneath his left foot. He stumbled, might have fallen had he not clutched at a thick, wooden beam standing at a tilt beside him. "Carmen, you okay?"

"No." Her voice was weak and trembling. "My leg's stuck, Damon. It won't budge. I'm trapped."

chapter
13

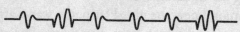

Arriving at Carmen's side, Damon knelt to aim his flashlight into a small crevice in the huge slab of rock pinioning her leg. The limb was firmly entrenched up to her upper thigh. Because she was wearing a skirt, her leg was bare from the knee down, and Damon could see that it was bleeding. Scraped by the stone, he figured. He hoped that was all it was. They were going to have a hard enough time getting her out of there without having to worry about a compound fracture.

"I wasn't hurt in the . . . explosion or whatever . . . it was," she explained. Her teeth were chattering with cold, sending her words forth in a jerking pattern. "I was leaving . . . the science library . . . I was almost out the door . . . and then there was this horrible noise . . . and I guess I was knocked out. I was okay when I came to, I think . . . just some bruises, and my head ached. After a while . . . I started to climb over all this junk . . . to get out of here. But I slipped, and my leg slid down inside here . . . and when I tried to pull it out . . . I couldn't."

That explained why she hadn't been crushed by the huge slab of stone. It was already on the ground when she arrived at this spot. Lucky girl. But she probably wasn't feeling very lucky right about now.

"Well, I guess we need to get you out of here, don't we?" Damon said lightly. "But first, I'm going to have a paramedic check you out, okay? Just to be safe. I wouldn't want to move you if you have any . . . well, anyway, let me call someone. This'll just take a minute." He knew that was a lie, but he wanted to cheer her up. He got to his feet and called for a medic.

Will responded, scrambling awkwardly over the rough surface, jump bag in hand. It was called a *jump bag* because when the paramedics jumped out of an ambulance, it was this bag they always carried with them. Damon knew it held necessary equipment for making a hasty preliminary diagnosis of a patient's condition — stethoscopes for listening to chest sounds, blood pressure cuffs, the drug book, an endotracheal setup — but he also knew there wasn't anything in that bag that would help them get Carmen out of the fix she was in.

Sam was right behind Will, his face and hands so covered with white dust, he was almost unrecognizable. There was a nasty cut on his left, ungloved hand where, Damon guessed, he had probably sliced it on stone. Some of the broken pieces were as sharp as knives. A thin stream of blood trailed from the laceration, turning pink as it mixed with the white grime. Sam seemed totally unaware of it.

"What've we got here?" Will asked as they arrived, and then he whistled low, under his breath. Recovering quickly, he smiled down at Carmen and asked, "Decided to take a nap, did you?"

Carmen, her face drawn, her teeth still chattering, managed a weak laugh. "I'm . . . really cold," she said shakily, but Will was already peeling off his fleece-lined jacket. He wrapped it around her, then moved a large chunk of stone behind her back to support her. She sank against it in relief and smiled gratefully, huddling deep inside the jacket's folds.

"So, what hurts?" he asked, removing a stethoscope and blood pressure equipment from the bag. He said to Damon, "Go get more help," and Damon was gone.

"I don't know," Carmen answered. "I think my leg hurts, but it's so cold now, I'm not sure." She raised her head, her long, dark hair tangled around her face, and gazed above her with fearful eyes. Will glanced up, too. With the second floor completely gone, they could see all the way up to the huge, jagged hole in the third floor. "I was almost outside the building," she said, "when it blew up. I guess the explosion threw me back inside. The rest of it isn't going to come down on top of us, is it, Will?"

"Nah. This was an old building. Solid as a rock." He laughed ruefully as he wrapped the blood pressure cuff around an upper arm. "Except for explosions, of course." Her blood pressure was slightly lower than it should have been. He couldn't see the cut on her leg well enough to gauge its severity. She could be losing blood. Better safe than sorry, he thought, and warmed a packet of IV solution under his sweater before inserting the needle in Carmen's arm and opening the line. "Anyway, the fire department's working on shoring up what's left of the third floor. We'll let them worry about that. All we want to do is get you out of here."

Other than her low blood pressure, her vital signs were stable. But Will knew the real dangers: shock and/or hypothermia. The latter would send her body temperature dropping to dangerous levels. She'd been sitting too long in the cold. They needed to get her out of there and under a warming blanket.

In an effort to make her slightly more comfortable, Will managed to insert a folded layer of gauze through the slit in the rock to give the leg wound some protection. He knew it wasn't enough, but Carmen thanked him and said bravely, "It feels better already."

Will didn't believe her.

Other paramedics and firemen arrived to help free the girl. It quickly became clear that it wasn't going to be an easy task. The chunk of solid stone pinioning Carmen's leg was enormous.

"There's no way we can risk bringing heavy equipment in here to get that off her," the Fire Captain told Will quietly. "Even a high-speed drill to cut through the rock would cause too much vibration. We'll have to think of something else."

They called in every available rescue worker, but even with the added man power, the stone refused to budge.

Will decided to try something else. If they couldn't move the stone, they would have to move Carmen. Removing a large syringe from his jump bag, he asked one of the firemen to bring him a can of motor oil. When Will had the can in hand, he loaded the oil directly into the syringe. Then he shot a spray of oil into the crevice, trying to avoid Carmen's leg, intending only to grease the sides of the rock so they would be able to pull the limb free.

That effort failed. No amount of tugging and pulling would budge the leg.

An ominous rumbling overhead brought Carmen's head up in alarm. "Please," she cried, "please get me out of here! Can't you *do* something!"

It was Damon's idea to try soap. On his instructions, Sam ran to the triage area, returning a moment later bearing a bottle of disinfectant soap.

The expression on Carmen's face, the way she bit into her lower lip when the foamy liquid accidentally soaked the gauze pad covering her leg wound, told them that it stung fiercely. But it worked. A few minutes later, the bloody leg slid free of its trap, and Carmen, released at last, sagged backward into Will's arms, crying with relief.

Will didn't like the way she looked. Her face was white with cold and shock. He didn't want to waste time taking her temperature until she was safely inside the warm ambulance, but her hands, when he touched them, felt like ice. "Let's move!" he ordered, and the shaking, crying girl was hastily lifted onto a stretcher and covered with blankets.

Dr. Izbecki wasted no time in triage. He took one look at Carmen and told Will, "You've already done the preliminary work. Transport her *now*."

As they hurried away, Damon turned to Sam. "You'd better go, too. Get that cut on your hand cleaned out and dressed before it gets infected."

Sam shrugged. "They can do that here, can't

they?" he said, gesturing toward the triage area.

Damon peered more closely at the injured hand and shook his head. "Nope. It's my guess that thing needs a stitch or two. Go on with Will. You can come back when the hand's been taken care of."

Susannah, seeing Sam move down the slope toward the ambulance, hurried after him. He explained, and she ran back to Abby. "I'm going with Sam. He's cut his hand. I'll drive his van. Anyway, I think I can do more good in ER. I'll come back later if they don't need me there. Call me if they find Jeremy, okay?"

Callie returned just as Susannah climbed into Sam's van. "Where are *they* going?" she asked Abby irritably. "I mean, the only reason I hung around here was because Sam was here. He's leaving?"

"He cut himself and needs stitches. Don't worry about it, Callie."

Muttering in disgust, Callie ran down the slope, back to The Beanery's parking lot, climbed into her robin's-egg-blue sportscar, and raced away with a squeal of her tires, following the ambulance.

It was worse in ER than Kate had expected. There seemed to be gurneys everywhere, all of them filled. The downsized staff was dashing from one cubicle to another, taking vital signs, whipping gauze pads free of crackling plastic envelopes, setting up IVs, wrapping blood pressure cuffs around arms.

"God, where do I start?" Kate breathed as a nurse flew by carrying blankets.

"Right here!" The pile of white was plunked into Kate's arms. "Take one of these to every treatment and trauma room. If you need more, go get more. These people were found outside the building. They're freezing. When you've delivered the blankets, find out which doctors need you the most, and do whatever they ask."

The problem the doctors were having, Kate realized as she went from room to room delivering the blankets, was deciding which to treat first: the hypothermia, or the broken bones and severe lacerations. The patients Kate saw were all shivering uncontrollably. Their answers to questions were slow and dull, and vague. Only two of the seven recent arrivals looked as if their injuries would not require surgery.

"It could be worse," Dr. Shumann commented, her eyes fixed on the cardiac monitor for a middle-aged woman with a serious head wound. "What we've seen so far is mild hypothermia. The lowest core temperature is ninety-three. A few degrees lower and these people would be shivering so violently it would be impossible to treat their wounds. I hope they get the rest of those people out of there quickly."

During that intense thirty-five-minute period

when all seven people were being treated at the same time, Kate saw dismaying proof that the explosion on campus had been a violent one. There were so many lacerations. Some were serious, some were not. There were also broken bones, four of which required surgery. Kate and an orderly whisked those patients upstairs to operating rooms, while the rest of the staff worked at disinfecting, stitching, and dressing deep lacerations.

When she wasn't taxiing patients upstairs, Kate held the suture tray for a doctor stitching up a cut dangerously close to an eye. The patient, a girl who was so terrified her head had to be restrained while the stitching took place, would not be discharged that night. Her blood pressure was dangerously low, and she was suffering from mild hypothermia.

Kate took her upstairs when the last stitch was in place. She guessed there would be a slight scar, hidden mostly by the girl's eyebrow. She'd been luckier than the woman who had been brought in with a similar but far more serious laceration on her cheek. That patient was in surgery now, being tended to by a plastic surgeon.

She held another tray while a different doctor, this one a young resident, pulled together the jagged edges of a laceration that ran from a young man's ankle all the way to just below his knee. He had been struck by a razor-sharp chunk of blackboard.

He had high praise for the paramedics who had rescued him. "I was afraid I was going to be spending the night out there," he told Kate. The local anesthetic injected into his leg kept him from feeling any pain. "But all of a sudden, there were these guys lifting that blackboard off me, and asking me how I was doing. One of them was that fireman who made the papers last year when he pulled Abby O'Connor's dad out of the refinery fire, remember? Damon Lawrence? I've never been so glad to see someone."

Kate felt a rush of warmth at the sound of Damon's name. She pushed it away. No time to think about him now, not now.

But she wondered if he'd found his father.

Then she stood by, making notes on a medical chart, while a gray-haired professor's earlobe, hanging by only a thin strip of skin, was sewn back into place. Because of the man's age, there were concerns about his blood pressure and heart rate, and Kate had been instructed to keep accurate notes as the nurse continued to monitor those vital functions.

Each time a patient had been treated, Kate thought of taking a minute to go to the house phone and call upstairs to ask Rosie Murphy if Margo had been located yet.

But they had barely finished with all seven when the pneumatic doors to the ER swung open and a new patient, a young girl with a bloody leg, arrived, with Sam and Susannah right behind her.

chapter
14

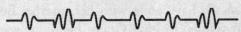

Jeremy heard the ambulance sirens fading away. They seemed to be taking his hopes of being rescued along with them.

I want to be in an ambulance, he thought with a deep pang of envy. Someone *else* was found. Several someones, maybe. Other people had been found and taken in nice, safe, warm ambulances to the nice, safe, warm hospital, where their cuts and bruises and headaches would be taken care of. Why not him? Why hadn't *he* been found?

He wondered if his father knew he was missing. Probably not. It would take the rescue people a while to find out exactly who had been inside the building when it blew, and who hadn't. By the time they tell him I'm among the victims, Jeremy thought, I'll probably already be safe inside his precious hospital.

But if he *wasn't* found soon, then there would have to be a phone call to San Francisco. To his mother. He wondered if she would cry when she heard the news. Probably. She'd always been very dramatic. He had liked that about her. It made her much more interesting than his father. Difficult to live with, because you never knew what might set her off, but interesting.

He still missed her. He could have gone with her, *should* have gone with her, maybe. But he hadn't wanted to leave Grant. He didn't want to start over somewhere else. It was hard enough to get along in Grant, never mind some strange, new place where he didn't know anyone.

Silly to think he might not be rescued. Of course he would be. Will would find him, or Damon Lawrence, maybe even Sam. They were probably all out there, hunting for him. He'd be found, just like those other people.

But it had better be soon.

Kate knew the girl brought in on a stretcher ahead of Susannah and Sam. Her name was Carmen Lopez. She was a cheerleader at Grant Regional High, a friendly, bright girl. But she didn't look so bright now, with her face as gray as stone and her bloody leg thrust out in front of her.

As if that weren't enough, Sam's left hand was wrapped in a bloodstained white cloth. While Will wheeled the injured girl off to one of the rooms, Kate unwrapped the cloth and took a look. The cut was nasty. "How did you do this?" she asked, leading him to a suture cubicle. Susannah, her face pinched with anxiety, followed.

There were no suture trays in the room. Kate had to go in search of one. She was pulling supplies from a cabinet in another room when Callie Matthews poked her head in. "Where did Sam go?"

Kate didn't even look up. Disgusting, the way Callie hounded Sam, when he clearly wasn't interested in her. Of course, it was his fault, too. He took the girl out whenever the impulse struck him, and that encouraged her. "You can't go in there. He's being stitched up."

Callie laughed rudely. "Well, aren't *you* the bossy one! I am *so* sick of people ordering me around. And you are *not* in charge here, Kate. I go where I please in this hospital. Don't forget, my father *runs* this place."

"Get out of my face, Callie. I'm busy. In case you haven't heard, we have an emergency on our hands, a very large one."

"I know. I was *there*. Sam won't be going back there, not with an injured hand, so I'm going to take him out to get something to eat as soon as they finish sewing him up."

"Don't be too sure." Kate turned around to face Callie. "He has a friend sick in this hospital, a girl, and I'm sure he'll want to go up and see her, now that he's here. He might even stay up there all night." She didn't add that the last she'd heard, that particular patient was missing. "So you might as well go home, Callie."

"Not on your life. I'm waiting right here for Sam. If he wants to go up and visit his little friend, I'll just go with him." She walked over and took a seat on a blue plastic bench.

While Dr. Shumann stitched up Sam's hand, Kate stood by, holding the suture tray and thinking about the different explosion theories proposed by those patients who were able to talk.

The girl with the cut under one eyebrow had said, "I think it was a bomb. I was just walking along, thinking about my date Saturday night, and all of a sudden, everything around me lit up, like there'd been one of those big bolts of lightning we get sometimes in the summer that light up the whole sky? But the sky was clear. There wasn't any storm. Only just for a minute, then, I *did* think storm, because there was this horrible roar that could have been thunder, only it was a lot louder, but I still thought just for a minute that it was thunder, and it was a storm. Then I knew it wasn't, and then my glasses exploded. I'm *sure* it was a bomb. It had to be."

But the boy with the leg laceration had scoffed at the idea of a bomb. "It was the furnace," he insisted. "That furnace was old. Ancient. I know, because one of my buddies does maintenance work in that building part-time to pick up a few bucks, and he was always complaining about that furnace. He said it was a safety hazard. It just finally blew up, that's all."

The professor whose earlobe was being reattached had had a different theory. "It was the Beech boy," he told Kate, the doctor, and the nurse in attendance. "The Beech boy."

Kate thought he had said "beach boy." There was no beach in Grant. "Excuse me?"

"Beech boy, Beech boy!" the professor repeated, clearly agitated. The resident had to warn him to sit perfectly still. "His first name is Timothy. Timothy Beech. He fancies himself a chemist, but I assure you, he is *not* one. I told John, Professor John Hawkins, Beech's chemistry professor, that he shouldn't let the boy have such free and easy access to the lab, but John just laughed off my concerns. He said Beech had an inquisitive mind and should be encouraged."

"Please, Professor," the resident pleaded, "you have got to sit still or you're going to end up with a very lopsided ear."

Ignoring him, the man continued, "Beech is in my ten o'clock. English lit, my subject, you know. And more than once, I had to stop him from disrupting my classes with his incessant bragging about his crazy scientific experiments."

As the resident continued to stitch painstakingly, the professor went on speaking, oblivious to the needle piercing his earlobe. "I know a thing or two about chemistry myself, and I saw some of Beech's equations. Most of them made little sense, and some of them were downright dangerous. I would be willing to wager my collection of first editions that the Beech boy is behind this. He was probably up in Hawkins's lab . . . it's on the second floor of the Science building, or *was*, and he was no doubt mixing together chemicals that proved to be volatile when combined. I can almost guarantee that's what took place." He waved an age-spotted hand. "And just *look* at the results!"

But, Kate had thought later as she'd ripped a bloodstained disposable sheet from an examination table, the *real* results haven't even arrived yet. There was probably worse to come, in the form of those people who'd been unlucky enough to be inside the building where Tim Beech had been at work.

So far, only Carmen Lopez fit that category. But at least she'd been conscious, with no serious head or chest injury.

But as the last stitch in Sam's hand was completed, he said, "Let me tell you something, it was a shock to uncover nine people at one time."

"You mean seven," Kate corrected. "Seven came in here."

Sam and Susannah exchanged a glance. "There were nine," Susannah said quietly. "Two didn't make it."

Kate was stunned. No one had told her. "Dead?" That made three, so far. Lars Pedersen and the two who hadn't even made it to the hospital. She thought of Damon's father. "Do you know who they were?"

"A guy name of Brown, from Eastridge, and a woman from the West Side."

Not Rowan Lawrence.

Kate had overheard a bitter argument between the father and son shortly after Rowan Lawrence had returned, unannounced, to Grant. The man had been brought into ER suffering from a severe allergy attack. He was pale and wheezing, his pulse rapid, his breath coming in short, shallow gasps. At first, the paramedics and Dr. Izbecki had suspected a cardiac incident. But then Damon had appeared in the doorway to inform the staff in a flat, unemotional voice that "Mr. Lawrence" (he had never once mentioned the word *father*) was severely allergic to animal dander, and the family had recently adopted a mutt from the Humane Society's shelter.

Mr. Lawrence was given a shot of epinephrine and released.

Kate had been in the lounge when she'd heard voices raised in the hallway. She had immediately recognized one as Damon's.

"If you think we're getting rid of the dog, you're crazier than I thought you were," he was saying loudly. "That dog'll be around long after you've taken another hike. When's that gonna be, anyway, Rowan? Next week? The week after that? Next month? It'll happen, and you and I both know that, don't we?"

"I'm not leavin' again," a deeper voice said staunchly. "I told your mama that and I'm tellin' you that, and I mean it. I'm home, Damon, and you'd best accept it."

Damon laughed scornfully. "Home? You don't have a clue what that means. That's *my* home. I was the one who fixed the roof when it leaked and painted the house when it peeled and cleaned it out after the floods. I helped pay the bills and I'm the one who was there when Jimmy needed something, but you weren't. Where were *you* when all that stuff went down? Nowhere around, am I right?"

"Yeah, you're right. And I'm sorry about that. I am truly sorry. But I mean to make it my home now. It's okay with your mama. I'd like it to be okay with you and your brother, too. I can't see that it's bothering him all that much."

"Jimmy's too little to stay mad for long. I'm older and smarter. And I see right through you, old man."

"No, that's where you're wrong, son. You don't see nothin' but what you want to see. And you are wrong."

Later, Kate had tried to ask Damon about the argument, but he'd refused to talk about it. She had a clearer picture now, though, of what it must have been like for him, feeling responsible for his mother and his brother, not even knowing where his father was, and hating him for not being there. Maybe he'd never even *wanted* to drop out of high school. She had thought he did it because he wanted to have fun. Maybe he hadn't had any choice. His mother couldn't make all that much money working at the refinery. The family must have needed money.

"What's it been like over here?" Susannah's voice asked from behind Kate. "Awful, I'll bet, am I right?"

Kate put Damon out of her mind and turned around to tell Susannah that, yes, she *was* right.

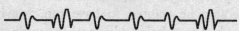

Because Sam was suffering from mild exposure, he was ordered to remain on the table under a warming blanket when his hand had been bandaged. He wasn't happy about this turn of events, but the doctor was insistent. Will, satisfied that Carmen was being taken care of, came in to see how Sam was, and decided to stay with him.

Telling Sam to rest, Kate and Susannah walked together to the staff lounge, where Kate poured two cups of hot coffee. The narrow, cluttered room was empty. Any staff member free at the moment had moved to the ER's waiting room to watch coverage of the disaster on television. "Here," Kate said, handing Susannah a cup. "You look like you could use this."

"Thanks. Anything hot is welcome." Susannah glanced through the doorway at Callie, still seated on the bench, swinging her red-booted legs. "What's she doing here?"

"Waiting to pounce on your poor, unsuspecting brother. She never blinked an eye when I told her Sam was worried about Margo. Callie got this look on her face like she'd never heard of the girl. Like she was thinking, Margo *who*? I almost laughed." In a more serious tone of voice, Kate filled Susannah in on the missing Margo. "I hope they found her. Hold on a sec while I call upstairs." She went to the phone, punched a few buttons, and then spoke. When she hung up, she was nodding. "They tracked her down. She was downstairs in the basement, in nothing but her johnny. That girl is so determined to get out of this place, I wouldn't be surprised if she tied a sheet to her bed and escaped through the window. If whatever ails her doesn't kill her, pneumonia surely will if she goes out on a night like this without a coat."

Susannah stared into her cup. "I just don't get it. She doesn't seem like the kind of girl my brother usually dates. He goes for the healthy, Nordic types. That wouldn't include Margo Porter."

"It used to," Kate pointed out. She sank down into the worn tweed couch. "I mean, Margo was once as healthy as you and I, remember?"

Susannah nodded. Leaning wearily against the peach-colored wall hung with bulletin boards, calendars, and schedules, she asked, "While we're waiting to find out how Carmen is, tell me what's been going on here. How bad was it, really?"

"Well, you already know about the passersby. They were hit by stone and flying glass. Lots of lacerations . . . some facial. We had to call a plastic surgeon in. He was at the country club, hadn't even heard about the blast. We had two head injuries, one serious. Then we had an English lit professor who was on his way to the building to pick up some papers and nearly lost an ear. He kept talking the whole time he was being stitched, all about how he thinks some kid blew up the building by mixing the wrong chemicals." Kate glanced up at Susannah. "Is that what the firemen say happened?"

Susannah nodded. "That's what the Fire Captain thinks. I keep wondering if Tim Beech might have caused the explosion. And if Jeremy was sitting right beside him when it happened. If he was . . ."

Kate stirred her coffee thoughtfully. "Did you know Lars Pedersen didn't make it?"

Susannah didn't recognize the name.

"That boy who came in earlier, from the site. He had a bad head injury? Blood clot. He died on the table."

"I hadn't heard." They sat silently for a few moments, then Susannah said, "Everyone's working so hard to get people out, but it's slow going." She walked over to toss her crumpled Styrofoam cup into a wastebasket, and leaned against the sink. "I think Carmen will be okay, don't you?"

"I think so." Kate leaned her head back against the couch. "Do you know if Damon's found his father? He thought Rowan was working in the Science building tonight."

Susannah shook her head. "Not as far as I know." Solemnly, she added, "That would be the pits, wouldn't it? His father just came back after being gone so long, and now he might be . . . hurt."

"I want to go see how Carmen is. And Will looked like he could use some coffee." Susannah poured the dark brown liquid. "You coming?"

Kate followed her to the treatment cubicle.

Although Carmen wasn't hypothermic, the girl was so chilled that Dr. Lincoln decided to keep her overnight. Will had returned. When Susannah and Kate entered and flanked him, he told them Sam was napping.

"He'll be mad," Susannah said, "when he wakes up. He's not a napper. Sam hates to miss anything. The only reason he sleeps at night is because everyone else does, so there's nothing exciting to do."

"Carmen's leg isn't broken," the doctor told them. She smiled down at the patient, lying quietly on the table, the leg neatly bandaged. "I'll have Fitzgerald take her upstairs. Grant, you call her family." To Carmen, she added, "If everything else checks out okay, you'll probably be sprung tomorrow."

Dr. Lincoln left to summon the orderly. Susannah stood beside the examination table, adjusting the blanket around Carmen's chest. She was still shivering with cold. "I guess it was pretty bad, being stuck like that," Susannah said sympathetically.

Carmen nodded, her dark eyes huge. "I've never been so scared. But at least my head wasn't covered up. I keep thinking, there have to be people under all that stone. *Buried!* That must feel so horrible, like being buried alive."

When Carmen had been taken upstairs, Susannah thought again of Jeremy. He could *be* one of those people Carmen was talking about. Buried alive, under all that cold, heavy stone. She tried to imagine how Jeremy would react to something so terrifying, and couldn't. Although she had known him since seventh grade, when they entered the same private day school together, Jeremy was a hard one to figure out. She never knew what he was thinking, not for sure.

When Jeremy's mother left, he hadn't even told anyone until three weeks later. Susannah had heard it first at the country club, when someone told her parents. "A writer?" her mother had said in disbelief. "Bianca is going to be a *writer*? Whatever for?"

Susannah had assumed at first that Jeremy hadn't told his friends because he was so hurt that his mother hadn't taken him with her. Then she'd learned, from Jeremy himself, that his mother had *asked* him to go to San Francisco with her, and he'd refused. Susannah hadn't known what to think. It was hard to know how to react to someone's problems if you didn't have a clue how *they* felt about them.

If Jeremy was out there in the cold, buried in stone, was he terrified? Did he feel abandoned, alone? Even if he was used to feeling that way, with his mother gone and his father too busy for him, this would be a very different kind of abandonment. Much more frightening, Susannah thought to herself. Had Jeremy already given up hope of being rescued, the way he'd given up hope of his mother ever coming back? He never even mentioned her name anymore.

Don't give up hope, Jeremy, Susannah directed silently. *Someone will find you. Someone will get you out.*

She hoped she was right.

In his black, icy prison, Jeremy slowly became aware that there was something very wrong with him. It was something more than just being trapped in this coffin of cold, rough stone. In some strange, bizarre way, he had almost become used to lying completely prone, unable to move, like a mummy swaddled in white. He had stopped expecting that at any moment, the coffin cover would be lifted, and a head would peer down into his hiding place and say cheerfully, "Well, what on earth are you doing in *there*?" That possibility no longer seemed as likely as it had at first. There was still noise around him, but that had been the case for some time now, and it hadn't seemed to do him any good.

He decided the problem was that he'd been lying in the same position, barely moving so much as a finger, for far too long. His head reeled dizzily, and he could no longer feel his toes or his fingers. They had tingled for a while, a sensation that for some reason had struck him as funny. But when he tried to laugh, his chest had expanded and rammed into the stone pressing down upon him. That hurt so intensely, he had strangled the laughter, swallowing it whole just as it was about to escape.

"The problem is," Jeremy murmured, his lips barely moving because they were so numb with cold, "you can't spend your whole life living with a doctor and not know something about medicine, no matter how hard you try. I think I'm getting frostbite. Guess I should have worn a hat or gloves or maybe boots. Not that the hat would still be on my head." He had to fight laughter again at the idea that a hat might have stayed on his head while he was being buried beneath who knew how many tons of rubble. "It is possible that if I'm not yanked out of here pretty damn quick, I could lose a finger or two, maybe a couple of toes."

If Jeremy had been thinking clearly, that thought would have terrified him. But because of the drop in his body temperature, his mind was no longer functioning at top form. He decided that it might be kind of interesting to be missing a digit or two. People would find that fascinating, wouldn't they? "Maybe I'll make the papers again," he murmured.

Jeremy had been in the local papers last summer for saving the life of a girl who had almost drowned in a private pool during the virus epidemic. His father hadn't even known his picture was in the newspaper until a secretary told him. Even then, all he'd said was, "Well, well, well! It's a good thing I taught you CPR, isn't it?"

Thinking about that now, Jeremy found the whole thing very funny. The one heroic thing he'd done in his life and his father wanted to take the credit. As if the eminent cardiologist Dr. Thomas Barlow didn't already get enough attention.

I needed credit for that rescue, Jeremy

thought, the laughter gone, anger taking its place. I needed him to be proud of *me* for a change.

He had an image of himself standing next to a brick wall, repeatedly smacking his head into it. That was how he felt when he tried to talk to his father. The image struck him as funny. And although it hurt each time his chest hit the rough stone above him, he let the laughter roll out and fill the narrow tunnel where he lay unseen and unheard. Just like always, he thought. Unseen and unheard and unnoticed. What's wrong with me? I should feel right at home here.

chapter
16

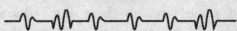

When Kate had gone upstairs to check on Margo, Susannah and Will were alone in the room. She glanced over at the navy blue jacket lying in a heap on a stool beside the door. She had known it was Will's the minute an orderly gently removed it from Carmen and tossed it on the stool. Carmen had already said Will was one of the people who had helped her, and Susannah knew that Will would never stand by and let someone freeze while he stayed cozy and comfortable in a warm, fleece-lined jacket.

Silently, she reached out and picked up the coat to hand it to Will, smiling up at him as she did so. "Here. You're going to need this if you're going back out there." Moving closer to stand directly in front of him, she added, "And you *are* going back over there, aren't you?" She didn't want him to. She wanted him to stay here, with her, where he was safe.

He nodded. Slipping into the jacket, he said, "They need all the help they can get. I take it you're staying here?"

"I think so. Kate said it was pretty horrendous when that group of seven came in. And I wasn't getting much done on campus. Kate's concerned about a friend of Sam's who was brought in today. She's in ICU upstairs, and if I stay, Kate can spend some time up there. But," she added quickly, "if you think, at any time, that I'm needed over there, if things start speeding up, call me on the radio, okay? I'll be there in two secs." A pang of fear stabbed her. After he left here, how would she know he was all right?

Noticing her sudden shudder of fear, Will took her hand and led her from the room, directing her to a dim corner in the lobby, behind a tall, potted plant. Facing her, he asked, "How many runs have I gone on, Susannah?"

Looking up at him questioningly, she answered, "I don't know. You were a paramedic before I even came to ER. Dozens? Maybe hundreds?"

He laughed. "No, not hundreds. I *do* go to school during the day, y'know. But I was at the refinery fire and came through that okay, and I went on runs during the flood and survived that. I guess I can handle a blast scene, especially since the blast already happened and I know I'm not about to be blown to pieces. There isn't any gas leak, you *did* hear that, right?"

"That doesn't mean it's not dangerous over there," Susannah persisted stubbornly. "You *know* it is, Will. Look at Carmen. She wasn't even hurt in the explosion, not really. A few bumps and bruises, maybe. She was hurt *after*-ward. The same thing could happen to you. You could just be walking along, searching for survivors, and slip on a pile of stone, maybe hit your head . . ." She was thinking blood clot, the very thing that had killed Lars Pedersen.

"Whoa!" Laughing, Will held up a hand. "I thought you were planning to become a doctor. Maybe you should rethink that idea. I'd hate to lose a good partner in my clinic, but you're sounding to me like a born writer. What an imagination. I'm *not* going to slip. Relax, Susannah. I'll be fine."

Fixing bright blue eyes on his, she said seriously, "Don't make fun of me for caring about you, Will Jackson."

His own voice grew equally thoughtful. "You think I'm making fun of you? Not even close." And without bothering to check and make sure no one was watching, he put a strong hand on either side of her face and bent his head to kiss her.

He had kissed her before. But this time, knowing he would be returning to the blast site — a dangerous excursion — Susannah wished the kiss would never end. Then Will would never leave the safety of the hospital and return to campus. She let her feelings for him take over

. . . no more thinking, no more analyzing about what their relationship meant . . . just pure, sweet emotion. If he *had* to go back over there, she at least wanted him to know that she'd be thinking of him while he was gone.

When he lifted his head, his eyes on hers were very dark, and he breathed softly, "I'll be okay over there, I promise."

"You'd better be." But she smiled as she said it.

The farthest thing from her mind was whether or not anyone might have seen them. She really didn't care at that point.

So when a thin, sly voice behind them said, "Oh, isn't that just too sweet for words? Young love in bloom, right here in little old Grant Memorial. I *love* it!" it took Susannah several seconds to connect the voice to Callie Matthews. When she had, her head dropped onto Will's chest and she groaned, "Oh, here we go again! Do you *send* for her before you kiss me?" Callie had caught them in a hug once before, but to Susannah's surprise, hadn't made a big deal about it. Susannah had finally decided that Callie was afraid Sam would be mad at her if she gossiped about his sister. She hadn't wanted to take that chance. But now, here she was again.

Will laughed. He reached down to tilt her chin upward, forcing her to look at him. "Do we care?" he asked. "Of all the people in the world, whose opinion do we care less about than Callie Matthews'?"

When she didn't answer, Will's voice deepened, and he wasn't smiling anymore. "Susannah? We *don't* care about Callie, do we?"

"No," she said quickly, "no, of course we don't." Then, because his eyes said that he wasn't sure she meant it, she turned to face Callie. "Just in case you think my cheeks are red with embarrassment," she said clearly, "they're not. They're red from being outside, in the cold. So when you tell your little story to anyone who will listen, make sure you add that Susannah Grant was not the least bit embarrassed to be caught kissing Will Jackson. Have you got that straight, Callie?"

"Well, sure," Callie said, smiling and bobbing her blonde head up and down. "Of course you're not embarrassed. Why would you be? This is the nineties, Susannah, and I've always said I thought Will Jackson was just about the cutest, nicest boy in all of Eastridge. I've said that, Susannah, you know I have."

Susannah wanted to gag at Callie's ingratiating manner. Falling all over herself now, pretending that she wasn't going to make a big deal about this, when all three of them knew perfectly well that she was. "You're wrong, Callie," she said smoothly. "Will's the cutest, nicest boy in *Grant*, not just Eastridge."

Callie smirked. "Well, of course *you* think that, Sooz."

Susannah winced. Only Abby called her *Sooz*.

Will took Susannah's elbow and hurried her to the door.

"She's going to fly upstairs on her broom and tell Mr. Matthews what she just saw," Will said, "and he'll pick up the phone and share the news with *your* parents. You *do* know that, right?"

"Um-hum. What's your point?"

"Your mother will have a stroke."

Susannah shook her head. "Let me tell you something about my mother. If you don't spit into your napkin at the table, and if you say please and thank you and pardon me and you like classical music and read a book once in a while and appreciate good art, she doesn't care where you live or how you dress or . . ."

"Or what color you are?" Will asked skeptically.

"Exactly. That's just who she is. She has these *standards*. I think she learned them at finishing school or something, or maybe from my grandmother. We were raised on them. They're more important to her than anything. *Standards* count. How you behave, that's what my mother cares about. Not wealth or position or breeding. Or race."

"Even in my case?"

"Even in your case. In *anyone's* case. Look at

156

who my best friend is, Will. Abby O'Connor. Abby doesn't have tons of money, and her parents don't belong to the country club, or go to the symphony or entertain fifty-five important people at a time like my parents do, and her house is crowded and noisy with all those kids, and the dog sheds all over the furniture. But my mother adores Abby, anyway. Abby isn't loud and vulgar, she covers her mouth when she coughs or sneezes, and she knows what a butter knife is for. So my mother doesn't care that the O'Connors aren't in the social register. That's just who my mother is."

Will looked wary. "Hard to believe. I'll bet the same thing isn't true of your father, is it?"

Susannah thought for a minute before answering honestly, "I don't know. I wish I did. Anyway," she added hastily, uneasy about the sudden, tense look on Will's face, "it doesn't matter. My dad and I have an understanding. He concentrates all of his attention on Sam and leaves me pretty much to my mother." She thought she managed to hide the pain in that remark very well.

But Will knew her. He reached out to pull her close to him again. "You *could* talk to him, you know. You could sit down and tell him how you feel about everything. I'll bet he'd listen."

Susannah pulled away. She did *not* want to discuss her relationship with her father. "Well, it won't be tonight. We have a crisis on our hands tonight. Have you forgotten?" She wouldn't blame him if he had. *Her* mind certainly had been wiped clean of everything but that kiss. "Speaking of which, you'd better get back over there. As much as I'd rather you stayed here where it's safe, I know you want to get back and help. I'll see you later, okay? And please let me know if you find Jeremy."

Giving her a quick kiss on the cheek and promising to call her on the radio, Will hurried away.

As she watched him go, Susannah put a hand to her lips, touching them gently, smiling as she felt again the sweetness of his kiss.

Then she remembered Callie standing in front of them, with that stupid smirk on her face. She probably already had raced upstairs to tell her father, who would almost certainly call Samuel Grant II to tell him what his daughter was up to at Med Center.

Maybe not. Caleb Matthews must have his hands full right about now. Maybe he wouldn't even listen to Callie's mad rantings.

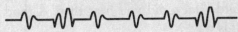

The only part of his body that Jeremy could move at all was his left foot. It was leaden from lack of movement, or maybe it was frostbitten, and he could barely feel it. But when he tried, tentatively, to move it upward, it seemed to be doing as instructed. He lifted it higher, higher, until the tip of his black loafer was touching the top of his prison. The pain in his thigh was almost unbearable. But he was afraid if he gave up and let the leg fall, he would never be able to raise it a second time.

Biting down hard on his lower lip to keep from screaming in pain, he began tapping on the rock with his foot. Tap, tap, tap, leather to stone. The sound it made was useless. Louder, he told the shoe, you have to be *louder*!

He summoned up every last ounce of strength he possessed. Gritting his teeth, he brought the foot down slightly, only an inch or so, and then swung it back up again, this time kicking at the stone with more force. He hit it hard, awakening his foot and toes. A shaft of pain shot all the way up his leg, so bone-numbing, his head spun, and he almost passed out. His left leg dropped harmlessly back to the bottom layer of the rock and rested there.

But from somewhere above him, he thought he heard, "Hey, did you hear that? A thud . . . over this way!"

Jeremy did scream then, but not from pain. He took a deep breath, and let out a scream for help that bounced off the walls and assailed his ears, nearly shattering his eardrums.

And then someone's voice, so close that Jeremy could hear every word, said, "There's someone under here. C'mon folks, let's dig 'em out!"

Satisfied, Jeremy closed his eyes.

At the same moment, another voice, much farther away, called, "We've got people here! Five of them. Medic!"

This time, when Kate went upstairs, Margo Porter was actually in her room. She was lying in bed in silence. No music, no magazine to read, just lying there staring up at the ceiling. The expression on her face was decidedly hostile, Kate thought as she entered.

"So, you're still here, after all." Kate sat on the edge of the bed. "I hear you tried to make another break for it. Curses, foiled again. Why don't you just stay put? And it's the middle of the night, Margo, why aren't you sleeping?"

"Because I *hate* it here!" Margo nervously fingered the edge of the sheet with bony fingers. She glanced up at the IV. "I'll probably weigh two hundred pounds by the time they let me leave. I don't see how they can keep me here against my will."

"You're a minor. Your parents make that decision. They want you to live."

"They want me to live *fat*. Anyway, they're getting a divorce."

"Your parents? They're divorcing?" Kate quickly reminded herself that this problem of Margo's had probably been coming on for a long time, and wasn't necessarily connected to her parents' situation. But eating disorders, Kate had been told last summer, were about control. If Margo felt she had no control over her family situation, maybe she'd settled on the one thing she *could* control, her food intake, to make her feel safe. So all that stuff about the gymnastics team had just been a smoke screen. It wasn't the real problem. "I'm sorry," Kate said gently.

Margo shrugged. Tears gathered in her eyes. "We'll be moving, my mom and me. We can't afford to keep the house I grew up in. I love that house. And I want to stay in Grant and graduate with my class. But we have to go back to my mother's hometown, Pasadena, California!" She laced the word *California* with contempt.

"If you don't want to go, couldn't you stay

with a friend here until you graduate? I know someone who did that when her folks divorced."

Margo looked up at her with solemn, pale blue eyes. "Not now. When I first found out they were talking about splitting up, last fall, I thought about finding a place to stay, here in town. But my mother had a fit. She said we have to stay together." She laughed bitterly. "Look who's talking about staying together! And now that I'm sick, I *have* to go with her."

"Then maybe you should try to get well so you *can* stay here. All you have to do is eat, Margo. That's not so hard, is it?"

But Kate knew, looking at the expression of alarm on Margo's face, that it was indeed hard. Maybe impossible. "You're not going to try to split again, are you? You're not stupid, Margo, you have to know how dangerous that is."

"Where's Sam?" the girl asked abruptly, turning her face away from Kate, into the pillow. "The nurse said he was in Emergency, that he'd cut his hand or something. She was going on and on about how good-looking he is. I could tell she didn't understand what he sees in *me*. Is he coming up to see me?"

"I think he is. He was suffering from exposure, so they're warming him up." Kate stood up to leave. "Can I get you anything before I leave?"

"Yeah, a robe. It's cold in here. My mother

brought mine, it's over there on that chair."
Margo gestured weakly.

The room, like most of the hospital rooms, was overheated. But Kate decided that someone with no fat whatsoever on her body for insulation might feel chilly even when it wasn't. So she brought the thick, pale pink robe over and helped Margo put it on.

The effort exhausted the girl. When she sank back on her pillow, Kate was satisfied that even if Margo wanted to run again, she'd never be able to get out of bed.

"Sam should be up soon. I'm not sure they'll let him in to see you, though. He's not family."

"You talk to the nurse, then. She'll listen to you. Tell her I really *need* to see Sam." A crafty expression crossed Margo's face. "Tell her if she lets me see him, I'll eat something."

Kate hesitated in the doorway. "But that wouldn't be true, would it, Margo?"

"Maybe." Margo's voice hardened. "But if he doesn't get in, I won't eat *anything*, you can tell her that, too."

Kate did tell Rosie what Margo had said, and talked the nurse into letting Sam visit for a few minutes. She knew the nurse wouldn't have given in if Sam wasn't the son of the most powerful man in town, but she didn't care. If Margo got what she wanted, maybe she wouldn't try to leave again, at least for a while.

"They've found more survivors," Nurse Murphy told her. "We just heard. They're bringing them out now. One of them is Dr. Barlow's kid."

Kate brightened. Good news, finally. "Jeremy? Really? Is he okay?"

"Don't know. You'll find out when you get downstairs. They should be bringing them into ER soon."

Anxious to give Susannah the news, Kate hurried to the elevator.

The news that six more survivors had been uncovered traveled quickly to the avenue. Shouts of approval rose up from the street, mixed with some murmurs of concern from friends and relatives awaiting word.

"Give us their names!" a man standing beside an ambulance shouted, moving forward a few steps. "Tell us who they are! We've been waiting a long time."

"Just be patient," a campus security officer told him, waving him back. "Let the doctors treat them. We'll give you their names as we get them."

A member of the press corps, seated atop a large white van with a television station's call letters on the side, shouted, "You haven't given us *anything* yet! All we've got is film, and we can't even get close enough to get a shot of any survivors. I can't write a story with nothing but film. I need information, man!"

The security guard turned away, calling over his shoulder, "You can follow the ambulances to the hospital. Maybe the paramedics will give you what you need. My job here is to keep you away from the site, and that's what I'm doing."

The grumbling subsided then, as six empty stretchers were rushed from the triage area over to the collapsed building.

The first of the six patients dug out of the rubble was a young female student whose only injuries were a broken ankle and several small cuts on the bridge of her nose. Will and his partner carried her to the yellow section of triage.

Watching, waiting with a tray of hot coffee for any of the survivors who were well enough to drink a warming liquid, Abby thought the girl had been incredibly lucky. She was shivering with cold, and crying with relief, but she was basically intact. "What happened?" she kept asking. "What happened?"

"They found Jeremy," Will told Abby quickly before he turned to leave again. "They're digging him out now."

"How bad is he?"

Will shook his head. "I don't know yet." And ran off to help.

Of the four other patients, three were brought

to the yellow area with broken bones — which were quickly splinted before they were removed by ambulance — and lacerations that required hospital care. The fourth, an elderly librarian, although not seriously injured by the explosion itself, had apparently suffered a massive coronary episode. She was already dead when they pulled her out of the debris. Attempts to revive her failed, and she was taken to the blue area.

Watching in dismay, Abby felt overwhelming fear for Jeremy. She wasn't afraid that he, too, had suffered a heart attack. Jeremy was young, and strong. But what were the chances that he had survived that terrible explosion? The Fire Captain believed the blast had taken place in the science lab . . . exactly where Jeremy had been headed when he left The Beanery. He could have been sitting right alongside Tim Beech when the room went up in smoke and flames.

She would have gone, then, to see for herself what kind of progress they were making in getting Jeremy out, but Astrid, busy at one of the cots, called to her, asking for coffee for one of the rescue workers who had stumbled into triage, exhausted and frozen to the bone.

Abby took the coffee and a roll to the man, wrapped a blanket around his shoulders, and sat with him while he filled her in on the status of their search. "The Fire Captain thinks there are only two or three more people left inside," he told her. "We'll get them out." He sipped the coffee gratefully. "If we don't freeze first."

"I'll take some coffee over there," she said, getting up. "Maybe that will help."

But before she could do that, Will and his partner arrived, carrying one of the survivors on a stretcher. The face was bruised and bloody and covered with white dust from the stone.

It was Jeremy.

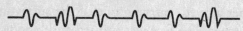

Abby knew the moment she entered the red triage area that Jeremy was in dire straits. Paramedics had pulled his jacket away from his neck and shoulders, and Abby could see the veins in his neck standing out, as if someone were pinching off his blood supply. His face had a bluish tinge to it, he was breathing too fast, and he was trying desperately to sit up.

He's hurt his chest, Abby thought. That scared her. Something was pinching his heart, stopping the flow of blood. He was already on oxygen, the mask over his face. She could hear him gasping, "My chest . . . my chest hurts, and my head."

Dr. Izbecki, stethoscope on Jeremy's chest, said cryptically, "We've got a developing tension pneumothorax here."

Abby's eyes widened, remembering the refresher course . . . Jeremy's lungs were collapsing? That could kill him.

A paramedic quickly hooked up the cardiac monitor, and Abby could see clearly the squiggly line on the screen. She didn't know what it meant until the doctor said, almost under his breath. "Sinus tachycardia with occasional premature ventricular contractions. Transport to hospital, stat!" Dr. Izbecki's head swung around to address two paramedics waiting for orders. Everyone else was busy taking care of the other five survivors, one in the red area, two in yellow, and two more in green. "You can do the IV on board. Listen to heart sounds as you go, and stay in constant touch with the hospital." He stood up, motioning toward the patient, still stirring restlessly on the cot. "Come on, let's go, let's go, let's *go*!"

Abby wasn't familiar with all of the medical terminology. But thanks to the refresher course, she did know that Jeremy had suffered a chest injury so severe that at least one lung was in danger of collapsing, and his heart, which had probably been injured in the blast, was not functioning normally.

And she knew enough to realize, as she ran and as Sid wheeled his chair alongside the gurney being rushed to an ambulance, that this friend of hers, so agitated, so pale under his oxygen mask, was in serious trouble.

"You'll be okay, Jeremy," she said, reaching for his hand. When she took it, she gasped. He wasn't wearing gloves, and his fingers felt like icicles. "They're taking you straight to Emsee. Susannah's there, she'll take care of you. Just hang on, okay?" He was sure to need emergency surgery when he got to the hospital. Abby wondered if his father would be allowed to perform it. She didn't think so. Not on a close relative. But Dr. Barlow would know someone else who could do it, another expert. Jeremy would get the best care possible.

Will and his partner thrust the gurney into the back of the ambulance. They jumped in, the doors closed, and the vehicle with Jeremy inside took off.

"Maybe I should have gone, too," Abby told Sid. There were tears in her eyes. Jeremy wasn't an easy person to figure out, but she knew enough about him to know that he was a good person. Unhappy, maybe, but never unkind. "It's bad, I know it is. Maybe he would have wanted me to come with him."

"Will's with him. And Susannah's at Med Center. You're needed here. Those other people they dug out might need some help."

They began moving back up the slope. People called out names to them, asking if they had seen a son, a daughter, a friend. Sid and Abby couldn't answer. Giving out that kind of information was up to the Crisis Intervention Team, a group made up of counselors, ministers, and city officials. "If the Fire Captain is right," Abby said, "most of the people are out now. So if those people down there are still missing someone, that person is probably just at a party or a movie or in a dorm room. What about this last group? How bad?" She'd been so preoccupied with Jeremy, she hadn't checked out the other survivors.

"Not too bad. Broken bones, deep cuts, maybe a concussion or two. Someone mentioned a fractured ankle. I heard they think there are only one or two more people unaccounted for." Paramedics ran by the two of them, hurrying down to the staging area to collect fresh supplies. "Damon's getting really uptight, I can tell. He hasn't found his father yet." The zipper on Sid's red athletic jacket had slipped open. When he yanked it back into place, Abby noticed with affection that his dark hair needed cutting. Maybe she'd do that tomorrow . . . when all of this was over. "The longer it takes, the less likely it is that he'll be okay." Sid reached across for her hand and looked up into her face. "How are *you* holding up?"

"Okay," Abby said. "How did you get your chair across all that rock? I saw you helping them lift that slab of stone away from that one group of people."

"Damon carried me. And Sam followed, with my chair." Sid laughed. "They said they needed my brute strength." He grinned up at Abby. "Maybe I have a career ahead of me as a furniture mover. Think it pays well?"

"You're going to be a football coach, remember?" The faces of the people standing in the green area awaiting treatment reflected shock and bewilderment, along with their cuts and bruises. Someone should tell them to sit down on the cots, Abby thought, before they *fall* down. "You'll be out of that chair eventually, and even if you aren't, it won't matter. You need brains to coach, not legs. No more talk about moving furniture, okay?"

Triage was bustling with activity as the patients were tended to. Before Sid returned to the blast site, Abby had to ask, "Do you think Jeremy will make it?"

"I don't know," Sid answered honestly. "He looked like he'd been run over by a train. Depends on how tough he is, I guess. You know him better than I do."

Abby thought about that. Was Jeremy "tough"? Was he made of strong stuff? "I think he can beat this," she said. "I think he can. Now give me a long, long kiss before you go over there and risk your gorgeous neck."

The kiss, which Sid was only too happy to deliver, helped keep Abby going as she busied herself filling out call sheets for the new arrivals in triage, and pouring hot coffee for weary, frozen rescue workers.

But she kept seeing Jeremy's face, so gray and pained, just before the ambulance doors had closed upon him.

When Susannah went to see how Sam was doing, she passed Astrid on her way out of the treatment room. The head nurse barely nodded at Susannah.

That seemed strange. But Susannah decided it was just that Kate's mother had a lot on her mind.

Sam was sitting up on the table, a gray blanket around his shoulders like a cape, layers of white swaddling the injured hand. "I had to have a tetanus shot," he said, grimacing and rubbing his upper arm. "Man, that hurt! I think she borrowed the needle from the elephant house at the zoo."

Susannah laughed and took a seat on the stool directly opposite Sam, beside a cart filled with medical supplies. "Why do you always act so tough? I knew that was an act. You had everybody fooled but your twin. How are you feeling?"

"Antsy. I need to get back to campus. Jeremy still hasn't been dug out."

Susannah was relieved to be able to tell him,

"Yes, he has. We just heard. They'll be bringing him in any minute now, so I can't stay. I just wanted to see how you were."

"They found him? Is he okay?"

"I don't know yet. I hope so. Dr. Barlow's on his way down to ER. Kate called him. He was in surgery, but he had someone else take over for him."

"They haven't found Damon's father, though, right?" Sam asked soberly. His cheekbones were still ruddy with cold, his eyes still heavy from his nap. "Will said Damon thinks he's in there somewhere." The tone of his voice changed then. "Listen, Susannah, about Will . . . you might want to think that over a little bit."

Susannah's jaw dropped. "Why do you listen to *anything* Callie Matthews tells you? You know how spiteful she is." Frowning, she added, "Anyway, you like Will, Sam. At least, I always thought you did. So what's the problem?"

Sam avoided her eyes, staring down at the white tiled floor instead. "It wasn't Callie who talked to me. It was Astrid. And I do like Will. But maybe you two should cool it for a while."

Callie had gone to Astrid about the kiss? How *dare* she! "I can't believe you're saying this! If I get my hands on Callie . . ."

"It's not Callie. Don't go laying this on her." Sam raised his head then, fixing an intent gaze on his twin. "Maybe you should be thinking about Will."

Susannah laughed. "Are you kidding? That's practically *all* I think about."

"Then think about *this*, Susannah. You're not risking anything here. Everyone in town knows you're Samuel Grant's daughter. So no one would dare say anything to you. But Will doesn't have the luxury of being protected by the Grant name. Do you really think things have changed so much that he can walk down the street with you and not be hassled about it? You're not that stupid."

Susannah jumped to her feet, her cheeks flaming. "I'm not stupid! And I'm not afraid."

Sam shook his head. "Well, maybe you should be. Not for yourself. For *him*. Jeez, you don't want to see him hassled, do you?"

"Will can take care of himself, Sam. You know that."

"I know. But I get around more in this city than you do," Sam said, sliding off the table and dropping the blanket. He tossed it on the table and slipped his heavy sweater over his head. "I'm *out* there a lot, and I can tell you, there are people here, just like there are everywhere, who won't tolerate Will walking down the street with a blonde-haired, blue-eyed female like yourself. They wouldn't like it at all."

Feeling defensive, Susannah said, "Kate doesn't feel that way. She says it's almost the twenty-first century. Will is one of her best friends. Wouldn't she say something if she thought we were a bad idea?"

Sam shrugged his shoulders. "Maybe she's as unrealistic as you are. Astrid isn't." He walked over to put an arm around Susannah. "Look, you think I like saying this stuff? I know it's stupid, and it's crazy, and it's not fair. But my gut feeling says I'm right. There's no reason why you can't be friends with Will. I'd just be really careful not to take it any further than that, that's all I'm saying. Not right now, anyway. Maybe later on."

Susannah knew he wouldn't be saying any of this if Callie hadn't told Astrid about the kiss. It hurt her that Astrid had gone to Sam. Why hadn't she come straight to Susannah?

Because she didn't *want* to hurt you, came the answer.

Shaking herself free of Sam's arm, she said coolly, "Kate says you should go up and see that girl Margo Porter. Margo knows you're in the hospital. You probably want to see her anyway, right?"

"No, not really." Sam walked to the doorway, stood there, looking glum. Blood from the cut on his hand was beginning to dry on the cuff of one sweater sleeve, and his hair was tousled from the pullover sweater. He looked like a little kid who'd just awakened from a nap. But the expression on his handsome face was that of an adult with something heavy on his mind. "She's got a ton of problems, that girl. More than I can handle. She didn't when I first met her, last summer at the club. She seemed fine. She wasn't any skinnier than any of the other gymnasts. But by Christmas, she'd changed a lot. I only saw her once in a while. We were both busy. And every time I did see her, she was thinner. I could tell she wasn't healthy. But she'd already become attached to me, and when I told her over the holidays that I thought of us as just friends, she went ballistic on me. She's real shaky, that girl. I'm not surprised she's in the hospital."

"You should go up and see her, Sam. Just as a friend, I mean."

Nodding, still glum, Sam said, "So, you're not mad at me, right? I mean, you know I just don't want anyone to bother you or Will."

Susannah knew he meant it. She hated everything that he'd said, but there hadn't been any meanness in it. "It's okay, Sam. Go see Margo. I need to think."

She meant to. But there was no time, because Sam had only been gone a second or two when Susannah heard the unmistakable wail of an approaching siren.

The things that Sam had said to her, curdling her heart and sinking her spirits, would have to wait. She'd think about them later. Right now, there were injured coming in from the blast site. They came first. Even before Will.

chapter 19

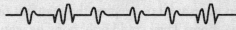

Susannah, Kate, several members of the medical staff, and Dr. Barlow were waiting anxiously under the canopy when the ambulance bringing Jeremy raced up the drive and screeched to a halt.

Will jumped from the back when the doors opened. He began rattling off vital statistics immediately, which instantly alerted the staff to the seriousness of the situation. Susannah heard, "BP seventy over fifty," and thought, oh, no! "He's had one thousand milliliters of Ringer's Lactate IV," Will continued. "It didn't do any good. We didn't use the antishock trousers because of the chest injury."

Dr. Barlow ran forward, grabbed the gurney the moment it was lifted out, and began running with it. The paramedics joined him and pushed, too. Still, it seemed to Susannah as she and Kate followed at top speed, that they were all going much too slowly, as if they were slogging through molasses. Time seemed so crucial. Jeremy looked terrible. Under the oxygen mask, she could see that his skin was colorless, and she could tell by the agitation he was displaying that he wasn't getting enough air.

Everyone in the ER knew this was the Chief Cardiologist's only son. They also knew there was no hope at all of keeping the man out of the trauma room. They could only hope he wouldn't get in the way.

He didn't. But Susannah noticed that he never took his eyes off the table where Jeremy lay. Drugs were injected. A tube was inserted into his nose to ease his labored breathing. Blood gases and X rays were taken. Another tube was inserted into his chest to reinflate the collapsing lung. Monitors beeped and chirped behind and beside him. All of this was done so quickly, Susannah had a hard time following it. But it was all only part of the battle. There was still the question of any damage to his heart.

"We're just wasting time here," Dr. Barlow burst out in an exasperated voice. "Let me take him upstairs now, before it's too late. Dr. Chan's up there, ready to operate."

Susannah, watching from a corner, held her breath. Dr. Barlow was technically more powerful than Dr. Lincoln. He'd been here longer than she had. It was hard to imagine anyone contradicting Jeremy's father.

"We need a CAT scan," Dr. Lincoln said stubbornly. She put her hand under Jeremy's head, and when she drew it back out, there was blood on her glove. "I want to make sure there's no intercranial bleeding before you take him up. You don't want to get him on the table and have him stroke out on you."

Susannah and Kate exchanged a glance. *His head, too?* the glance seemed to say. *Isn't it enough that he has a chest injury?*

Dr. Barlow not only agreed to the brain X ray, he insisted on pushing the gurney to the elevator himself. Everyone in the room would have agreed that he was behaving like a loving, concerned parent. Susannah found herself hoping that Jeremy was alert enough, in spite of his pain, to notice how worried his father was. Maybe that would make him feel better.

When the elevator doors had closed upon the small group taking Jeremy upstairs, Susannah let out a huge sigh and turned to Will. "We're not going to know for a while, are we?"

He shook his head. "Probably not."

"He's the worst case we've had in here tonight," Kate commented gloomily. "Except for Lars Pedersen."

"Which one was he?" Will asked. He was talking to Kate, but his eyes were on Susannah. She could feel his gaze, but she was remembering Sam's remarks, and couldn't bring herself to look up.

"One of the first ones brought in from the

area around the building. He didn't make it."

"Oh. I hadn't heard. I thought they'd all survived." Will glanced up at the big, round clock high up on the wall over Susannah's head. "It's only four A.M.? Man, it feels like we've been out there for days." He reached up to rub the back of his neck. "You been busy here with other stuff?"

Kate shook her head. She moved over to the table and began picking up medical equipment to return to the proper place in the cabinet. "No. The only good thing about tonight is that everyone is over on campus, they're not out driving around. We had one premature labor, two cardiacs, a kid who fell out of the top bunk bed and cracked his skull on a pair of ice skates on the floor, but that's about it. Everything else came from the blast."

Will nodded, lost in thought.

"I can't think about anything but Jeremy right now," Susannah exclaimed. "It's awful not knowing what's happening up there. Maybe I'll go up and check."

"There are two more ambulances on their way in," Will said. "Nothing major. Three people needing stitches and casts."

Susannah continued to avoid his eyes. "Kate's here. If it's nothing major . . . I really want to find out if Jeremy's okay."

"Yeah, sure. I've gotta get back. I need to help Damon find his father."

Kate stopped what she was doing to glance up. "He hasn't found him yet?"

"He hadn't when I left."

"Maybe Mr. Lawrence wasn't there. Damon wasn't that positive."

"If they don't find him soon," Will said, motioning to Susannah to leave with him, "he'll be frozen solid. And what's left of the third floor is making some pretty scary noises. I don't think they've had much luck shoring it up. The sooner we get the last of those people out of there, the better off everyone will be. C'mon," he said to Susannah, "I'll walk you out."

Susannah's mind raced. Was Sam right? If she allowed her relationship with Will to develop into more than friendship, would she be putting him on the spot? Not from any of *their* friends, she knew that. But Grant was a good-sized city. She didn't know half the people in it. Sam *did*. Were there really people out there who would become angry enough at the sight of her with Will that they'd give him a hard time?

"You don't have to walk me to the elevator," she said. "I know you're in a hurry to get back." She was not at all aware that her tone of voice had changed since that afternoon. It had been warm when she told him good-bye after the kiss, and full of promise. Now, it was cool and distant. "You go ahead. I'll just help Kate here, and then I'll go up and find out about Jeremy."

There was a long, pained silence in the room.

Kate, watching both of them, cleared her throat and said, "I think we need more adhesive tape in here. I'll go get it."

When she had gone, Will said quietly, "Susannah? What's going on?"

She turned away from him, her fingers playing with the handle on the cabinet drawer. "I *told* you, all I can think about now is Jeremy. He's *your* friend, too, Will. I'd think you'd be too concerned about him to think about anything else."

Another long silence. Then, "Right. You're absolutely right."

Although she hadn't heard the coolness in her own voice, she heard it clearly in his.

"Call me on the radio when you hear how he is, okay? See you."

She knew without turning that he was gone. Tears of fatigue and frustration stung her eyes. She had hurt him. She'd heard it in his voice.

But there was more than one way to hurt someone. Maybe this was better than the kind of hurt that Astrid was worried about, that Sam had warned her about. Swiping at her eyes with the sleeve of her pink smock, Susannah went upstairs to see how Jeremy was doing.

Margo was delighted to see Sam. She sat up in bed, beaming, holding out a hand toward him as he approached the bed. "Wow, you look terrible!" she cried, directing him to sit down on the bed. "Worse than me. It must be awful. Ambulances have been screaming outside all night long." She leaned forward, her pinched, white face peering up into his. "You've gotta get me out of here, Sam. You're the only one who can. I can't *stay* here. What happened to your hand?"

"Nothing, it's nothing." Sam slid backward slightly on the bed. "Look, Margo, I'm not even supposed to be in here. I'm not a relative. Kate got me in. What are you talking about, get you out of here? You're sick. This is where you should be."

Margo brushed a wave of dark hair back from her face. "I'm not sick. I'm just not . . . hungry, that's all, and they're forcing me to eat. It's disgusting. I don't have any rights at all in here. Listen, Sam, if you'll just get me out of here, I'll eat a seven-course meal the minute I'm free of this place, I promise."

Sam shook his head. "No way." His tone was emphatic. "They brought you here for a reason. Quit acting like a four-year-old and do what the doctors and nurses tell you. It's the only way you're going to get better, Margo. Look, I've gotta go. There are a couple more people still inside that building. They need me over there."

Margo sank back against the pillow. "My father's in there."

Sam was already standing, poised to leave. "What?"

"My father." Margo turned her head away from him, as if she didn't want him to see her tears. "I'm so frantic about him, I couldn't possibly eat anything. That's why my parents aren't here, Sam. My mother's over there, waiting to see if he's okay when they dig him out. I should be with her. I know she's scared to death."

"I thought you said your parents weren't getting along."

Margo sat up, her face eagerly turned up toward him. "That's right, they weren't. But she was really frantic when she heard about the explosion. She told me he was doing some research in the science library when the building blew up. She said she just *had* to be there, waiting, and she knew I would understand." She reached out for Sam's uninjured hand again, held it in both of hers, her eyes pleading. "See, I know, Sam, if my mother and I are both there, waiting, when they bring my father out, he'll see how much we both love him, and everything will be all right again. There won't be any divorce, and I can stay in Grant. So just take me over to campus, okay? You can drop me off in the crowd" — she gestured toward the television set high on one wall, tuned to the blast site — "and I'll find my mom while you get back to rescuing people. Please, Sam! This is really important."

A mixture of suspicion and doubt crossed Sam's face. "Your father's a lawyer. Why would he be doing research in the science library?"

"For . . . for a chemical company. They hired him to sue some suppliers. I swear it's the truth, Sam. We can sneak out the back way, go down the fire stairs. No one will see us. Anyway, when people know *why* I left, they'll understand."

"No. My father would disown me if he knew I helped a patient escape from the hospital. It's crazy, Margo! You need to be here."

Tears filled her eyes. "Then I won't eat. I can't. Not with my father missing and my mother waiting for him all alone, frantic over his safety, and worried about me at the same time. If I were there, at least she wouldn't have to worry about me, and I could comfort her while we're waiting."

Sam liked Margo's mother. She was warm and friendly, easy to be around. He'd been sorry when Margo told him about the impending divorce. If Margo was right, if this crisis was likely to turn the family around . . . maybe Margo would straighten up and get over whatever was wrong with her.

"You don't have any clothes," he pointed out, stalling for time while he tried to decide if this crazy plan of hers was a good idea or a bad one. "It's freezing outside."

"I have my robe. It has a hood. And I have

slippers." Her eyes glittering with hope, Margo snatched up the edge of the blanket. "I'll take this with me. It's wool, warm as a coat. And you always have extra jackets in your van. I'll put on one of those, I promise."

Most of the people who knew Sam Grant III well would have said he was sophisticated, savvy, maybe even a little cynical. But the notion of re-uniting a family that was splintering apart in-trigued him. If he hadn't been concerned about Margo's health, he would have said yes immedi-ately.

"You'll wrap up in the blanket? What about your IV?"

"Oh, that, that's no big deal," Margo said, and in a split second, she had yanked the needle and the tape free, pulled the hood of her pink terry cloth robe up over her head, and slipped the use-less pink slippers on her feet. She grabbed the blanket off the bed and threw it around her shoulders, then looked up at Sam expectantly, a happy smile on her bony face. "My parents will be so grateful to you, Sam, honest! I'm sorry the building blew up, that's really horrible, but this could fix everything between them. Let's go!"

"You sure your father's trapped in that build-ing?" he asked one more time. "I don't remember anyone at the site mentioning his name. They talked about a couple of the professors maybe being in there, and said Damon's father might be, but no one said anything about Rick Porter."

Margo looked up at him with wide, innocent eyes. "Sam. Would I make up something so awful? Do you really think I'd leave this nice, warm hospital on such a cold night if it wasn't absolutely essential?" She turned away, scooted quickly in her pink slippers to the doorway, and peered out. "There's no one there. Come on, hurry! I'll show you where the stairs are."

Doubt still in his face, Sam followed.

Two minutes after they'd disappeared into the stairwell, an attractive couple in casual clothing entered the room.

"Oh, no," the woman said, sagging against the doorframe. "Rick, she's gone again!"

"We never should have left her alone," the man said, his lips tightening in anger. "I *told* you, we needed to keep an eye on her. If her parents won't do that, who will? It wouldn't kill you to listen to me once in a while. But, oh no, *you* know everything! And now our daughter is missing again."

chapter
20

"**N**o word yet," Dr. Barlow's plump, red-haired surgical nurse, dressed in street clothes, told Susannah. She was sitting on a bench in Surgery's waiting room. "Thomas isn't operating, but they let him observe. He said I could go home, but I decided to stay. I like Jeremy. He's a nice kid." She looked Susannah up and down. "You're Samuel Grant's daughter. One of the twins. Are you Jeremy's girlfriend? Such a good-looking boy, isn't he? Doesn't look anything like his father, though. He's got Bianca's looks. She always was a beauty."

"I'm just a friend." Susannah sat down in a wicker corner chair. There was no one else in the waiting room. Only emergency surgeries, like Jeremy's, took place in the middle of the night. Relatives of those blast survivors who had required surgery had already gone home or were standing vigil in the patient's hospital room, waiting for the anesthetic to wear off.

This part of the hospital was eerily quiet, the

lights dim, the temperature sharply cool. She wished she had worn a warmer sweater under her smock. Still, full-body fatigue had begun to set in. Cozy warmth would have made it harder to resist sleep.

A television set on a low table in the corner was on, the sound off. The picture was the site on campus. Some enterprising news cameraman was using a zoom lens and had a very clear shot of the scene.

Susannah sat up straighter. "Have they brought any more people out?"

"Isn't this just awful?" the nurse murmured, her eyes on the set. Then Susannah's question registered, and she turned her head to say, "I don't think so. I had the sound on for a minute. The Fire Captain was being interviewed. He sounded really worried about the rest of the building collapsing on the rescue workers. He said he thought there were only one or two people still inside, and they were going to try to get them out as fast as possible." Then her eyes returned to the set and she repeated, "Isn't this just awful?"

Susannah saw her father, standing off to one side, his head bent, conferring with a member of the Crisis Intervention Team. She wasn't surprised. Samuel Grant II had probably left for the blast scene the moment he heard about it. Her mother was probably there, too, handing out hot coffee or moving through the waiting crowd to console anxious relatives. Her parents would never sit at home doing nothing while their city was in crisis.

She was about to lean back in her chair when the picture switched to two rescue workers, one in a fireman's yellow slicker and black helmet, the other in a paramedic's jacket. Though the camera hadn't zoomed in for a close-up shot, she knew instantly that she was looking at Will and Damon. Armed with flashlights, they were crawling through a narrow opening between two towering piles of debris.

"Is it snowing?" the nurse, watching, asked. "Doesn't it look like it's started snowing?"

Susannah peered at the screen intently. "No. That's not snow. It's stuff floating down from above them. From the third floor. Or what's left of it. You can just barely see the firemen working up there, trying to shore up the rafters. They must be knocking free dust or dirt."

"Looks dangerous to me," the nurse commented. "Both above *and* below."

Susannah agreed. Will, she messaged silently to the screen, get *out* of there! Let Damon find his *own* father.

She was immediately ashamed. I didn't mean it, she told herself, I'm just scared for Will. *No* one should be digging around in such a hazardous area.

She let herself be heartened by the nurse's report that only one or two people were still left inside. That had to mean that Will would be out of there soon, and safely back in ER.

And then what, Susannah? an inner voice queried. *Where do you and Will go from here?*

Just friends? she answered, sinking back into the chair, her eyes remaining fixed on the television screen.

Isn't it weird, though, the voice persisted, that you and Will can be friends and that's okay, but the minute it looks like you're more than that, some people get upset? It's not because you're rich and Will isn't. You could walk down the street holding hands with a white guy who was poor, maybe someone who grew up along the riverbank in west Grant, and no one would think a thing about it. But if Sam is right, it would be a different story if it was Will holding your hand.

Susannah thought wearily, Makes no sense to me.

Dr. Barlow startled them by appearing suddenly in the doorway. "Jeremy's heart stopped twice on the table," he said, sounding exhausted. He pulled off his green surgical cap and dropped his considerable bulk into a chair opposite the nurse. "Dr. Chan brought him back. He's a good man. I couldn't have done better myself." He leaned back in the chair, absentmindedly twirling the cap in his hands. "He'll make it," he added softly. "Jeremy. He'll be in ICU for a while, but he's going to make it." He looked at the nurse, then at Susannah. She thought she saw tears in his eyes, but wasn't positive. "Almost lost him this time. Came really close. I don't know what I'd do if that happened."

And are you going to tell Jeremy that? Susannah wondered. Probably not. She knew Dr. Barlow very well. She knew how busy he was. And when he wasn't busy with medical matters, he was at the country club golfing or entertaining friends. And because Jeremy was quiet and didn't complain much, Dr. Barlow assumed that meant his son was just fine. In the Barlow household, only the squeaky wheels got oiled, and Jeremy wasn't a squeaker.

Maybe you *should* be, Jeremy, Susannah thought. You could take lessons from Callie. She's an expert. Aloud, she said, "I'm glad he's going to be okay. He must have been terrified, buried in all that mess. And cold."

Dr. Barlow nodded. "His feet were mildly frostbitten. But that's been taken care of. They'll be fine. He won't be losing any toes." He pulled himself to his feet. "*He'll* be fine. Chip off the old block, Jeremy is. He's a fighter, just like his old man."

Oh, he is not, Susannah almost said. He isn't anything like you. He's artistic and creative and sweet and shy and if he's a chip off anyone's block, it's his mother's. He doesn't want to be a doctor, like you. The only reason he was even *in* that science lab was, he thought it would please *you* if he became a medical researcher.

"I have to go call his mother," the doctor said. He sighed heavily. "She'll blame me, of course. And she'll want to come here. But that would just make it harder on Jeremy when she went away again, don't you think? And she *will* do that. She won't stay here, with us."

Susannah thought he sounded a little wistful. Susannah had known the Barlows almost all of her life, and never once in all that time had she seen a look of uncertainty on the doctor's ruddy face. Unlike Jeremy, he had always seemed su-premely self-confident. But he looked uncertain now. He really *didn't* know what to do.

"Jeremy would probably like to see his mother while he's recuperating," the nurse said, standing up. "If he's going to be with us here at Memorial for a while, as you said, maybe she could come for a weekend visit."

Dr. Barlow nodded absentmindedly, which told Susannah that he wasn't really listening and he'd make up his own mind about parental visitation. He asked Susannah to say hello to her father for him, and left the waiting room.

The nurse prepared to leave, too. "Have you been here all night?" she asked as she picked up her coat and slipped it on. "You kids don't usually work nights, do you?"

"No." Susannah waved a hand toward the television set. "It's because of . . . what happened on campus. I was over there for a while, but I didn't think I was being very useful. Then they started bringing people out, so I came back here. I thought I could help more in ER."

"Terrible thing, terrible thing," the nurse intoned as she left the room.

Susannah sat for a few more minutes, watching television coverage of the rescue efforts. She wanted to stay, to do nothing but sit there and watch until she was positive Will was safe. But there was nothing she could do for Jeremy here, and she might be needed in ER. Reminding herself that there was a television set in the ER waiting room, Susannah pulled herself slowly to her feet and, with one last glance at the image of the paramedic and the fireman who were cautiously exploring the blast debris, Susannah followed the nurse out of the room.

* * *

"He's gotta be in here somewhere," Damon muttered, kicking aside a large chunk of stone with one booted foot. Raising his voice, he called again, "Rowan? Rowan, you in here? Make a noise if you can't yell for help. Scratch or pound or kick something, so we can find you!"

The only response he got was a creaking sound from above, followed by a shower of wood chips and sawdust. He didn't even bother to glance up. Half the time during their explorations, they were directly underneath the hole in the third-floor ceiling. The other half, they were sheltered from it by large chunks of broken stone slanted to provide a "roof" over their heads. He had to admit he preferred those moments, when they were under the protective umbrellas of debris, even though it meant walking hunched over like old men, sometimes even crawling on hands and knees. He didn't feel quite as exposed then.

"We've covered every inch of this section," Will said. He sounded exhausted. His hands and face were filthy with stone residue. The white dust rimmed his eyes, nose, and mouth, paled his eyebrows and hair. "There's no one in here." Cautiously straddling two chunks of rock, Will glanced around. They were surrounded by other rescue workers moving carefully but as quickly as possible from one square foot of space to the next, using their flashlights to see, stopping periodically to listen for sounds of distress. "Where should we look next?"

Although Damon couldn't bring himself to admit it aloud, he was becoming increasingly worried about Rowan. The last few survivors who had been uncovered had been suffering from hypothermia. What were his chances? He seemed healthy enough. He wasn't even that old. Early forties. Not old at all.

A soft, whispering sound to the left of him brought Damon's head up. His first thought was rats, but then he quickly decided there wouldn't be any rodents at the site just yet. That would come later.

The sound came again, louder this time. Without saying anything to Will, Damon moved to the left. There was nothing to see but more layered debris, and he could no longer hear the whispering sound.

Then he saw the foot. It was poking out from beneath thick sheets of flooring, lying at an angle just ahead of him. The shoe was old, black, the imitation leather cracked.

Damon knew that shoe. One of the first things he'd noticed about Rowan Lawrence when he had unexpectedly reappeared was, whatever else his father had been doing during all those years when he was gone, he hadn't been getting rich. The worn, tired shoes he'd had on, one of which Damon was staring at now, had told the whole story.

"Will!" he shouted, even as he bent to begin prying up the broken pieces of flooring covering his father. "Over here! I've found my . . . it's Rowan!"

chapter
21

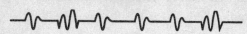

Sam wrestled with his conscience the entire time he was sneaking Margo out of the hospital. All the way down the stairs and into the basement, with Margo leading the way, the blanket wrapped around her shoulders trailing out behind her, he kept his eyes on her. He saw how weak her steps were, how her uninjured hand trembled on the railing, how she stumbled twice as they were descending, and almost fell.

As they neared the basement door, he thought clearly, she shouldn't be leaving the hospital. But then he remembered *why* she felt compelled to leave, and it seemed to him that it would be cruel to keep her here when her family needed her. If *his* father was trapped in that wreck of a building, nothing would keep him away. Doing what she asked might even improve her health a little bit. He'd just have to keep her warm. He could do that much. He had jackets in the van. And the second they knew her father was okay, he'd bring her back to the hospital himself.

They made it to the van without running into

anyone. The moon was still out, lighting up the medical complex's tall brick and stone buildings like a giant spotlight. The temperature had dropped several degrees. Sam scooped Margo up in his arms in the doorway and carried her across the parking lot. He was surprised by how little she weighed. Margo was seventeen years old, an athlete, and yet he might have been carrying a small child. Was she really that thin? Maybe she was sicker than he'd thought.

When they reached the silver van, he hesitated. Looking down at her blanket-bundled form and pale face, he asked, "Are you sure you want to do this?"

"I'm sure," she said. No hesitation in *her* voice. "I'm not cold, Sam. Quit worrying."

But when they were safely inside the van, he made her don a blue parka he pulled from the backseat, and a pair of heavy white socks he dug out of his gym bag.

"There!" she said when she was wearing the jacket and the socks. "Now I'm nice and cozy. Let's go!"

Sam started the engine. When he glanced over at her, he almost laughed. Margo had disappeared inside the oversized parka hood as if she'd backed into a dark cave. If it hadn't been for the pallor of her face, he wouldn't have been able to see her at all.

Her cheerful chatter as he drove to the blast

site puzzled him. She seemed to have forgotten that her father was in grave danger, her mother frantic with worry. She rattled on and on about gymnastics and an upcoming exhibition that she said she was sure to win, and then changed the subject to a Valentine's Day dance, talking about it in such a way that it was obvious she was wangling for an invitation. From him.

Sam was concentrating so hard on how to get out of asking her to the dance, he didn't notice at first that her words were slowly becoming spaced farther and farther apart, or that her breath was beginning to come in short, ragged gasps.

"I . . . think I'm going to . . . get a new dress . . . a red one . . . just for the . . . dance. I'll be better . . . then . . . and out of the . . . hospital . . . and . . ."

He *did* notice, however, when she stopped speaking completely. Surprised that she hadn't finished the sentence, Sam glanced over. He was horrified to find Margo slumped down in her seat. Her eyes were open, but her head lolled like a rag doll's against the seat. Without checking to see if anyone was behind him, Sam slammed on the brakes. The van screeched to a halt in the middle of the street. He reached over and grabbed her shoulder, calling her name, asking her what was wrong.

She couldn't answer. She tried, turning her

head toward him and opening her mouth. But she said nothing. She was ghostly white. The injured arm slipped from its sling and moved stiffly to her chest. She rapped the cast against it, as if that would make her heart do what she wanted.

"Oh, god," Sam groaned. "I never should have taken you out of the hospital! Hang on, just hang on!"

In a swift, expert move, he whipped the wheel around. The van, its tires screaming, made a wide circle until it was facing back toward the hospital. Then Sam stomped down on the accelerator and, hunched over the wheel in anxiety, drove as fast as he dared back to Grant Memorial.

Kate had planned to go upstairs to see how Margo was, but before she could do that, the emergency room, after a night busy primarily with the survivors of the blast, suddenly saw a burst of activity that caught both Susannah and Kate by surprise. An elderly woman, getting up in the middle of the night for a drink of water, had fallen, striking the back of her skull on a radiator. Although the blow had done no serious damage, the hot metal had burned her scalp. Her husband had brought her in. She was cheerful, complaining only that some of her hair had burned off and she'd have to change her hairstyle for a while.

But while she was on the exam table, she suddenly went into cardiac arrest.

A nurse began yanking open drawers in the crash cart while another covered the defibrillator paddles — intended to electrically stimulate the woman's heart back into a normal rhythm — with blue gel. Dr. Lincoln grabbed the paddles, shouted, "Clear!" and everyone stood back from the table while the patient was jolted with three hundred-watt seconds of electricity. The woman's body jerked, and a second later, the monitor showed a normal sinus rhythm.

A huge sigh of relief circled the table.

"What happened?" the patient's husband asked in a hushed voice. "What's wrong?"

"Nothing," Susannah said cheerfully, "your wife's going to be fine. They'll put some ointment on the head burn, and maybe you can take her home then."

She had barely finished the sentence when a nurse called, "She's crashing again!"

The entire process was repeated two more times. After the second stoppage of the woman's heart, Susannah was sent to the telephone to call Dr. Barlow, who was still keeping a vigil in his son's room in ICU.

While they were waiting for him, the husband, an elderly man with thick, white hair, became frantic. Susannah and Kate had to escort him gently from the room, leading him to the waiting room, where Kate poured him a cup of coffee.

He took the coffee, but didn't drink it, staring down into it as if it could tell him exactly why his normal night of sleep had been rudely interrupted. When Susannah attempted to extract information for his wife's medical chart, he was no help. All he seemed able to say was, "She just bumped her head, she just bumped her head," in a bewildered voice.

When it became apparent that the worried man was in no shape to answer questions, Susannah and Kate persuaded him to take a seat, their own eyes on the television screen on an opposite wall. Again, there was no sound, but the picture seemed much clearer. In spite of the lateness of the hour and the frigid temperatures outside, the crowd was as dense as before, and rescue workers were still searching through the wreckage.

Susannah couldn't make out Will or Damon, or Sam, whom she supposed was back on the site by now.

They had barely taken seats in the empty waiting room when another ambulance arrived, bringing five victims of a house fire caused by a defective space heater. Deciding the elderly gentleman shouldn't be left alone, Kate volunteered to stay with him while Susannah helped with the five.

All five family members had been overcome by smoke and were in bad shape. The youngest was only four. Susannah held his hand while he was given oxygen to combat carbon monoxide poisoning from smoke inhalation. His burns were doused with saline solution and dressed temporarily, in preparation for his transfer through the covered passageway that led to the Burn Unit on the grounds. The mother's burns were the most severe. According to the fireman who arrived with them, the mother had raced back inside the house to rescue her youngest child, an infant, before the fire truck arrived. The skin on her left cheek looked like it was dirty, but Susannah knew that what she was looking at was burn damage. The young mother would need plastic surgery. Fortunately for her, Med Center employed some of the best plastic surgeons in the world.

Treating five victims at the same time without a full staff, after a tense, anxious night, strained the doctors and nurses alike. Although there had been no fatalities, the family's tragedy further sobered everyone in ER. No one in the hospital ever became accustomed to the sight of a burned child, and their spirits had already been sagging because of the deaths and injuries at the blast site. A dismal quiet settled over the area.

"It's almost morning," Kate said desultorily as Susannah joined her in the waiting room.

Susannah went straight to the elderly gentleman slumped in a chair, his hat in his hands. She noticed then that he was wearing only worn brown slippers, without socks. A sign of the rush he'd been in to get help for his wife. "She's going to be okay," she told him, "but our cardiologist, Dr. Barlow, wants to keep her upstairs in ICU overnight, just to make sure there's nothing seriously wrong with her heart. I'll show you where you can wait, if you want."

As the man pulled himself to his feet, repeating, "She just bumped her head," Susannah tilted her head toward the television set and asked Kate, "Anything new over there?"

"Nope. It's kind of hard to see. I thought I saw Damon for a minute, but then he disappeared. Moved into a dark corner, so I can't tell what he's doing. Digging, I think. Will looks like he's trying to get to him, and can't. There's too much junk in the way. But he keeps trying."

"Well, I hope he's careful," Susannah said, and led the man away.

They had just disappeared inside the elevator when the Emergency doors flew open and Sam rushed in, carrying a limp, blanket-wrapped bundle. Kate felt the gust of cold wind and looked up even before he began shouting. "Help me here, someone! I don't think she's breathing!"

Kate knew who was in Sam's arms even before she jumped to her feet and ran, arriving at Sam's side along with a nurse and an orderly pushing a gurney. She saw the pink slippers, worn now over thick, white socks, poking out from beneath the edge of the blanket. Margo Porter had left the hospital, after all, just as she'd threatened to.

Sam must have found her wandering around, and had the good sense to bring her straight back to the hospital.

"No pulse," the nurse announced, signaling an orderly to bring a gurney.

Kate stood there motionless, thinking that she probably should do something, but unable to think what that might be.

Margo wasn't breathing.

"Hey, man," Damon shouted across the site to Will, "I could use some help over here. Looks like most of the building landed right here. And I don't think Rowan's the only one underneath all this stuff. I see the edge of a skirt, and what looks like a man's tie. There might be a couple more people under here. You coming?"

Will was trying to do two things at once. He was trying very hard not to wonder why Susannah's tone of voice had changed so abruptly, because he knew if he thought about that when he was also trying to make his way across uncertain terrain, he might make a mistake and lose his footing. It took every ounce of discipline he had, every ounce of determination, to blot out the sound of the voice, so cool, so distant, coming from lips that had, only a short while earlier, been soft and warm under his own.

Maybe she was worried about Callie. But Callie hadn't told anyone the last time she'd seen them together. She was too worried about what Sam would say. So what was Susannah's problem?

Well, what did you expect? Will asked himself bitterly. She's a Grant. You're a Jackson.

Never mind that now, his professionalism as a paramedic dictated. Pay attention to what you're doing, before you break your stupid neck!

Every time Will's foot landed on a new pile of broken stone, the beams above him creaked ominously again, and a shower of fine sawdust drifted down, some of it landing in his eyes. But he kept going. Damon needed his help.

"Will? You on your way over here, man? I can't do this by myself. This stuff's too heavy."

Aiming his flashlight ahead of him, Will searched with his eyes for a solid spot in the broken stone and wood around him. Finding it, he lifted his booted foot, about to take the step that would bring him closer to Damon.

His foot was in midstep when there came a horrendous groaning, creaking, splitting sound from somewhere high above him, and a distant, panic-stricken voice shouted, "It's going, it's *going*!"

Even before his head shot up, Will sensed what was happening. The rest of the third floor was collapsing. And he was standing out in the open, directly beneath the huge, cracked beam.

Sucking in his breath, he looked up to see the beam, split now into two. The frighteningly thick, broad chunks of wood were descending at astonishing speed, directly down upon him.

When the elderly gentleman had been settled into a comfortable chair in the ICU waiting room, the television on, a mug of steaming tea in his trembling hands, Susannah went back downstairs. It seemed to her the night would never end. When she passed the double ER doors, she could see faint edges of silver tinging the sky outside, signaling the arrival of dawn. The lobby was deserted, although she thought she heard a flurry of activity in one of the trauma rooms.

Before she went to check it out, she felt compelled to grab a quick look at the blast scene on the television set in the ER waiting room.

When she arrived in the doorway, her eyes went directly to the screen. She saw Will, standing in the midst of the rubble alone. But he wasn't digging. His head was up, his eyes on the hole directly above him, his arms extended as if he were reaching out for something to hold on to.

It all happened so quickly. One minute Will was there, right in front of her eyes. The next minute, twin, heavy beams were plunging down upon him. They landed in a cloud of smoky debris. And then Will was gone.

Susannah screamed.

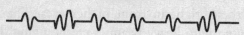

In the trauma room, the medical staff worked frantically to restore Margo's breathing. A nurse had jumped onto the gurney out in the hall, straddling the patient to begin CPR. She continued her efforts while another nurse administered oxygen, hooked up an IV, and took blood.

Kate and Sam stood against the wall, anxiously awaiting an update on Margo's condition.

"It's a good thing you found her," Kate said softly. "Where was she?"

Sam didn't answer immediately. Finally, his eyes still on the patient, he said, "I didn't *find* her. She was with me. I took her out of here."

"Stop CPR," Dr. Lincoln ordered after several tense moments, "I've got a pulse."

The nurse climbed down. "This girl is a patient here," Dr. Lincoln said when she had placed her stethoscope against Margo's chest for the fourth time in as many minutes. "What was she doing out of the hospital?" She ordered, in rapid sequence, several medications to be inserted into the IV. When no one answered her question, she added, "She is severely dehydrated. I repeat, what was she doing out of ICU?"

Sam, white-faced, stood near the door, against the wall, his arms folded over his chest. "I took her out," he admitted reluctantly. "Her father was caught in that blast on campus, and Margo was worried sick. . . ."

"Oh, excuse me, reality check here," Kate interrupted. "Her *father* is upstairs. He's perfectly fine, in the best of health, and so is her mother. Healthy enough to be arguing constantly. Margo lied to you to get you to spring her. And it worked, didn't it?"

Sam's handsome face flushed scarlet. "Her father's okay?"

Kate nodded. "Of course he is. But I'm not too sure about *you*," she added tartly.

"Well, I don't care *whose* son you are," Dr. Lincoln said sharply, "you might have killed this girl!" She covered Margo with a thick, white blanket, gently tucking the edges up under her chin. The girl's eyes were still closed, but Kate could see her chest rising and falling in a normal breathing pattern.

Kate took pity on Sam then and moved to his side. "Look, I know how convincing Margo Porter can be," she said quietly. "She wanted out of here, and she used you. It's really not her fault. She's very sick."

"I feel like an idiot."

"You *are* an idiot," Kate said mildly. "But you did the right thing, bringing her back here so fast. She'd have died if you hadn't. She hasn't been eating, and all of her vital organs, including her heart, are starving along with the rest of her. That's why she quit breathing. Anorexics like Margo are only thinking about what shows on the *outside*. They never think about the vital organs inside of them shriveling up from a lack of nutrition."

"We'll keep her right here for a while," Dr. Lincoln said, "where we can keep an eye on her. And keep that warming blanket on her. She's not hypothermic, so Sir Galahad here," she said, regarding Sam with a censoring eye, "must have at least seen to it that she was properly garbed. As for ICU, I'm beginning to wonder about just how *intensive* the care up there really is."

Kate felt a pang of sympathy for Rosie Murphy. It wasn't her fault. Margo was so determined to leave the hospital, an army of guards probably couldn't have kept her there.

"Anorexic?" Sam asked Kate as they left the room. "That's what Margo's got, anorexia? How could an athlete have that?"

"Oh, Sam, you *are* an idiot," Kate said affectionately, and would have laughed if Susannah hadn't appeared suddenly in the doorway. The look on her face scared both of them into utter silence.

Kate was the first to ask, "What? What's happened?"

Susannah struggled to speak. But she was fighting tears, and had to swallow those before she could speak. "Will. It's Will. I just saw" — she pointed behind her with a trembling finger — "on TV, the third floor . . . it gave . . . Will was right underneath it."

"Oh, my god!" Kate cried and, pulling Susannah along with her, ran to the waiting room. Sam ran with them. They burst into the room to find three nurses, two orderlies, and a maintenance man with a mop in his hand gathered around the set. Someone had turned the sound on, and an announcer's voice was saying, " . . . have no way of knowing if any rescue workers have survived this latest disaster."

A choked sob escaped Susannah's lips.

"Let me repeat for anyone just tuning in," the announcer continued unemotionally. "In the first gloom of dawn, there has been a further collapse of the Science building on the Grant University campus. We have been told that all but three of the victims trapped inside the building in the initial explosion already have been removed to safety, with three fatalities reported at this time. However, there *were* rescue workers still searching among the debris when the remainder of the badly damaged third floor collapsed on the site. We have not been given a list of names. We will update you further the moment we have more information."

Susannah stared up at the beautiful but blank face of the newscaster. How could she *say* something like that without blinking a single artificial eyelash? How *dare* she talk about Will like that, as if he were just a faceless, nameless *victim*? Will was *somebody*, somebody important.

"Oh, god," Kate said softly, turning to face Susannah with wide eyes, "Damon? Was Damon still *in* there?"

"I don't know. I only saw Will." Susannah's own eyes filled with tears. "He was standing right underneath that floor when it went, Kate. I *saw* it fall on him! *All* of it!" She shuddered. "It was horrible!"

Sam put a comforting arm around her shoulders. "You know Will," he said firmly. "If anyone could survive something like that, Will could. Just don't go jumping to conclusions, okay?"

"I have to get over there," Susannah said, swiping at her eyes with the back of her hand. "Sam, you have to take me over there."

"I want to go, too," Kate said. "The last time we saw Will and Damon, they were together. Damon could be hurt. I want to go see."

The two girls looked at each other. "We can't both go," Susannah said. "And Damon wasn't with Will when those beams caved. At least, I didn't see him there. Will was alone." Susannah's voice gathered speed, "I know it's not fair, because you've been here all night and you should be able to go, but please, Kate, please, I have to be there for Will." She was remembering the look on his face the last time she saw him. She'd hurt him badly, and out of what? Fear! Never mind that it was fear for *him*, it had still been cowardly of her. She should have been willing to face anything with Will, and she hadn't been.

She wanted the chance to tell him she was sorry. But those huge beams had been headed straight for him, and then he'd disappeared.

"Okay," Kate said, giving in. "But you owe me, Grant, remember that. And you can only go if you promise me faithfully that you'll find out, right away, if Damon's okay. Then call me."

"I promise. And thanks, Kate."

As they shrugged into their coats, Sam asked Kate for the second time, "You'll keep an eye on Margo?"

Kate groaned. "Like that's such an easy thing! If they can't keep track of her upstairs, what makes you think I can?"

"Just try, okay? She really scared ten years off my life, passing out in the car like that."

"Well, then, that makes you only seven years old now and you shouldn't be driving," Kate joked. But she actually felt like crying. She wanted to go, too, to be there for Damon if he needed her.

Then she remembered that she didn't *want* Damon to need her. So maybe it was a good thing that she wasn't going. She might be so glad to see him alive and in one piece, she'd say something really idiotic, something she couldn't take back later, when all of this was over.

Waving good-bye as Sam and Susannah pulled away, Kate turned and, telling herself that yes, it was a good thing she'd decided to stay here, went back to Margo's trauma room.

Damon stood staring in shock at the spot where, only seconds before, Will had been standing. In his place, broken wooden beams formed a kind of tepee. There was no sign of Will.

Torn, Damon struggled with his feelings. His father . . . Rowan . . . was buried beneath the pile of debris at his feet, and probably two other people, as well. But Will, who, although Damon had never told anyone, had been his hero for some time, was buried in another pile just ahead of him. He couldn't dig for two people at the same time. Impossible.

Rowan had been buried the longest. He could be close to death by now. He had to be desperately in need of fluids and warming. Minutes, even seconds, counted.

The very second the dust settled, other rescue workers began rushing to Will's aid. But that didn't erase Damon's dilemma. He knew he could call to those workers and ask them to dig *here*, where he stood, so that he could go to Will's aid. Should he do that? Let someone else get Rowan out? He didn't owe the man anything, not a thing, and he owed Will a lot. Will would have denied that, but Damon knew better. Every time he ran into Will Jackson after he'd had to drop out of high school, Will had nagged him about getting an education, had pushed him to get his GED, even continued to talk about the two of them going to college together, like they'd planned all along . . . until Damon had finally realized he had about as much chance of paying tuition as he did of sprouting wings. He'd given up then. But Will had never given up on him.

The realization that Will might not have survived the onslaught of those heavy wooden beams caused Damon's insides to twist in pain. "Oh, man," he cried softly, shaking his head and fighting angry tears, unaware that he was praying, "this can't happen."

Damon struggled to clear his head. What would Will do?

The answer came immediately. Every other available rescue worker was struggling to pull the heavy load of debris away from Will. Which meant that Damon was all Rowan had. Bitter laughter burned Damon's lips. Rowan Lawrence's chances of survival, good or bad, hinged on the son who didn't think much of him. That was pretty funny, if you stopped to think about it.

Damon didn't stop to think about it. Instead, with one last glance to confirm that Will had enough help, he began digging again to uncover his buried father.

chapter
23

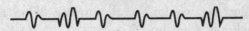

When Susannah and Sam arrived on campus, he didn't waste a moment searching for a parking space. The avenue was so thick with onlookers and emergency vehicles, they would have wasted an eternity searching for a proper space. Instead, he pulled up in front of The Beanery, next to a black-and-white sign that said clearly, NO PARKING, and stopped. "So it gets towed," he said, and they jumped out and ran.

"Have they found Will yet?" Susannah demanded of Abby when she located her in the triage area.

Abby's face crumpled. She was cold and tired, and she had witnessed with her own eyes the collapse of the third floor. "Oh, Susannah," she cried softly, "I'm sorry, I'm so sorry!"

Thinking she meant that Will was dead, Susannah gasped and sagged against Sam.

Abby realized her mistake. Instantly contrite, she said quickly, "Oh, no, no, I'm sorry, I didn't mean that. I just meant I'm sorry it happened,

221

that's all. No, they haven't dug him out yet. But it just happened a little bit ago, Susannah. They'll get him out."

Weak with relief, Susannah continued to let Sam support her. She was so drained, she was sure her legs wouldn't work, anyway. "Does anybody know if he's hurt?"

Abby shook her hooded head. "I don't think so. Not yet. But," she added heartily, "Damon's found some people, and they're all alive. His father, and some girl, and an older man. They're bringing them out now. I don't know how bad the injuries are."

"I want to help dig for Will," Susannah said emphatically.

"You can't. They won't let you, Susannah. Let the rescue workers do it. They know what they're doing."

Susannah's voice rose an octave. "I *want* to help dig! I can't just hang around here and do nothing. I'm going over there, and I'm going to *find* Will!" And she would have left then, if Sam hadn't grabbed her elbow and stopped her.

"Calm down," he said quietly. "You can't go in there. Besides, you heard Abby. They're bringing in three people. You can help right here. Will would want you to, Susannah."

Mentioning Will's name helped. "Okay, okay." Susannah took a deep breath and let it out.

"You're right, I guess. Whatever. I'll work here instead. That way, I'll be here the minute they bring Will out."

As they waited for the newest survivors to arrive, Abby and Sam exchanged a worried glance that said, *if* they bring Will out.

Damon's face and hands were grimy with white dust and smeared with blood from half a dozen cuts, but when paramedics had transported Rowan and the other two survivors to triage, he insisted on returning to the site to dig for Will.

"Damon," Susannah said gently, remembering that Kate had asked her to watch out for him, "you really should rest. You've been working a long time without resting. At least take a few minutes to drink some coffee. It's freezing cold out here. Dr. Izbecki said you all have to keep taking in warm fluids to ward off exposure."

Glancing down at his father, lying unconscious on a cot in the yellow area, his face bruised and bleeding, Damon said, "I have to help Will." He lifted his head then, looked at Susannah with bloodshot, dust-rimmed eyes. "You probably wish you could dig for him, too, right?"

He said it so calmly, so matter-of-factly, that Susannah realized he knew how she felt about Will. Maybe Kate had told him. Or maybe he'd seen them together and had figured it out for himself. It seemed perfectly okay with him that she cared about Will.

But then, Sam probably hadn't had Damon in mind when he'd warned her away from Will. Damon was Will's friend. He would never hurt Will's feelings.

It didn't matter now *who* Sam had been talking about. It wasn't important. All that mattered was finding Will, and having Will be okay. If he was okay, she could face anything. Anything at all. Astrid Thompson would just have to accept that. She cared about Will, too, or she wouldn't have said anything to Sam in the first place. Astrid would want Will to be happy.

And *I* make him happy, Susannah thought clearly.

"So, he's going to be okay, right?" Damon asked, pointing toward his father.

Susannah glanced over to the yellow area. "Yep, looks that way." She smiled a wan smile at Damon. "You saved his life. Your mother and brother will be really proud of you, Damon. You should be proud of yourself."

"Yeah, right. The old guy would probably leave me his entire fortune in his will now, if he *had* one."

In spite of the cynical remark, Susannah was convinced that Damon was at least a little pleased with himself. If he hadn't been worried about Will, she had a feeling he would have been more relaxed than he had since she'd first met him.

He drank the coffee in one gulp, and then he was gone.

The most seriously injured of the three wasn't Rowan Lawrence. He had a mild concussion and was suffering from shock and mild hypothermia. He was a very lucky man. The other man who had been found with him and taken to the yellow area had a broken arm, a fractured ankle, and was suffering from more severe hypothermia. He was trembling so violently, splinting his broken bones was virtually impossible.

"You'll have to warm him up first," Dr. Izbecki told the paramedics. "Forget the bones for now. Sandbag him so he doesn't do any further damage, then concentrate on warming his body temperature."

The most seriously injured survivor was a girl who, according to the driver's license they found in her purse, was eighteen years old, a student at the University.

"This one's critical," Dr. Izbecki announced. He saw to it that she was quickly dispatched to Med Center. When they had gone, he said to an exhausted-looking Astrid, "I wouldn't give any great odds on that kid making it." He glanced around the triage area. "Is that it?"

She nodded. "I think so. The Fire Captain thinks that's the last of them. Except for Will."

Susannah overheard her, and echoed the thought with a pang. Except for Will . . . except for Will, she would still be as lonely as she'd been when she started volunteering at Emsee. She shouldn't have let Sam's warning sway her. Will wouldn't have. Will wasn't afraid of anything. Except maybe her father, and that was only because he didn't know him. She would have to fix that. It was time. Dinner, maybe, at Linden Hall, or, if Will would be more comfortable, at a nice restaurant in town.

She would invite him as soon as he was found, dusted off, and standing upright again, smiling at her as if to say, "What? You thought I'd desert you, leave you out here to run that clinic in Eastridge all by yourself? That would never happen. You know me better than that, Susannah."

You wouldn't leave me if you could help it, Susannah told him silently, watching the last three survivors being loaded into ambulances on the avenue below. But what if you couldn't *help* it?

Resisting a shudder of fear that threatened to overtake her, Susannah went to ask Astrid if she could call Kate on the radio. She wanted to tell her that Damon was okay. She had promised.

Kate was cool about it, saying only, "Well, that's good." But Susannah knew Kate was secretly rejoicing.

When she had explained that Damon's father

was on his way in, along with two other patients, Kate asked, "And Will? What about Will?"

Susannah couldn't answer. The tears she'd been resisting forever had finally won out. She sat on a cot in triage, crying quietly, one hand on the radio, the other covering her eyes.

chapter
24

Kate did what she could to lift Susannah's spirits. But she knew in her heart that the only thing that would accomplish that was the sight of Will walking out of the wreckage safe and sound. And if not walking, then carried out, but not critically injured.

She stayed on the radio as long as she could, saying everything she could think of to cheer Susannah, because she really wanted to make her feel better. But she knew it wasn't doing much good. She could hear the quiet tears from the other end. And then the wail of sirens sounded from the back entrance, and she had to say, "Incoming's here. Talk to you later. Feel better, okay? Will's going to be fine," and sign off.

Kate's heart ached for Susannah, and for Will, as she joined the staff hurrying toward the ambulances drawing up outside.

She recognized Damon's father immediately, in spite of what the explosion had done to his face.

"Damon dug him out," a paramedic told her, knowing that Kate was friends with Damon. "Dug him out practically with his bare hands, while everyone else was hunting for Will. Must have been scary, uncovering your own father."

Yes, Kate thought, it must have been. Damon, she thought warmly, you are really coming along nicely. Might even be a great man someday.

She found herself hoping, just a little bit, that she'd be there to see it happen.

Rowan Lawrence was taken to a trauma room and placed in the care of Dr. Shumann. The broken bones case was handed over to an orthopedic specialist who had already been alerted, while the girl with the serious chest injury was whisked into Dr. Lincoln's trauma room.

They tried. They tried everything. Eighteen years old . . . hadn't even really lived yet . . . so much ahead of her. . . .

"She's ventilating!" one of the nurses cried only seconds after they'd begun working on the badly injured girl.

The crash cart was already in attendance. "Paddles!" Dr. Lincoln ordered. Gel was smeared, the call for one hundred fifty volts was sounded, the paddles were applied to the girl's chest. The table on which she lay jerked as the current hit.

Nothing. No response.

Kate, watching in apprehension, heard a soft whisper from behind her, "Oh, god, what's happening?"

She turned to see a white-faced, pink-robed Margo standing in the doorway. This time, she had brought her IV pole with her. She reminded Kate of Little Bo-Peep, all in pink, and dragging her sheep's crook along beside her.

"Get *out* of here!" Kate hissed. "Go away! What are you doing out of bed? You're supposed to be resting."

"The lidocaine's not working. Hit her again." The doctor's voice was tense. "This girl is only eighteen. Give me three hundred. Clear. Stand back!"

"She's not dying, is she?" Margo whispered behind Kate. "I know her. That's Casey Brook. Her younger sister, Tanya, is on the intermediate team at school. She can't *die*. She's only a year older than me."

Tense and tired and worried about Will, Kate whirled on Margo. She kept her voice low and restrained, but she put emphasis into every single word. "People *die*, Margo! They die from illnesses, they die in car wrecks, and they die in fires and floods and explosions. And *sometimes*," she added, her eyes on the pale face staring at her, "they die because they're too stupid to *eat*!"

Kate was sorry immediately. She hadn't meant to be so cruel. But it was the truth, wasn't it? On the table lay a girl who wasn't going to live to see her nineteenth birthday, would never get married and have children or a career, all because someone had been careless with chemicals. And in front of her stood a girl who was also dying. She was just doing it more slowly, and it wasn't somebody else's doing. It was her own.

She knew it wasn't that simple. Margo couldn't help it. But it seemed like such a waste, such a terrible waste.

Margo's face crumpled as Kate spoke, and her eyes began melting into a wash of tears.

"One more time! Three-fifty! Clear!"

One of the nurses declared, "No pulse."

The monitor screen showed a cruel flat line.

The room swam in silence.

"I could open the chest and begin massage," Dr. Lincoln said to no one in particular. "We might manage to keep this girl alive for a day or two, give her relatives a chance to say good-bye. But I suspect there is so much damage to the heart, she'll code again, and there'll be no saving her. I believe it would be kinder to let this child go now, in peace."

Eventually, the normal, heavy silence that always followed death in the ER began to break up, as it always did, slowly, like ice melting on a chilly spring day. Dr. Lincoln left the room, and the nurses performed their necessary tasks.

Margo, still crying, tugged on Kate's elbow,

pulling her out of the room. When they were in the hall, she sagged against the wall and said in a heartbreakingly weary voice, "I don't want to die, Kate. I *don't*. It's . . . it looked awful, what happened to that girl in there. I don't want that to happen to me. You have to help."

Kate inhaled sharply. Had she heard correctly? Margo was asking for help?

"I can't help you, Margo," she was forced to say. "I'm just a volunteer here in ER. You need doctors and nurses. You need an eating disorder program." She braced herself for the expected argument, but it didn't come.

"I know. But I thought maybe *you* could help. I mean, you work here, you must have heard things, like which programs work best and which ones don't. Please, Kate!" Margo was pleading now, still crying, her pale face pinking up with emotion. "Haven't you heard anything?"

Kate was torn. She *had* heard something. There was a program in Canada. She'd seen the woman on television. She had seemed gentle and loving and caring, and for those patients who stayed in the program, she had an impeccable success rate. But it's not my place to give medical advice, Kate told herself. Someone else here must know about that program. I can't be the only one who saw that story on television.

But what if no one else involved in Margo's care had seen it? What if they didn't know about it? She might end up enrolled in a program that wasn't nearly as successful.

Kate made up her mind. Putting an arm around Margo's waist to help support her, she said, "Let's get you back upstairs first. Then I'll talk to Rosie Murphy, and your parents, and your doctors, and I'll bet they can come up with something." It wouldn't hurt to just *mention* the Canadian program. Just in case Margo's doctors hadn't already heard about it. The girl wanted to live, didn't she? They owed it to her to make sure she got the chance to do that.

"Have you ever been to Canada?" she couldn't help asking as they stepped into the elevator. "I hear it's really pretty."

There were no patients left in triage, nothing for Susannah to do to help pass the time. She sat on a cot, hands in her lap, never taking her eyes off the site where a dozen or more rescue workers were shoveling and digging and tossing rubble this way and that in their search for Will Jackson. Daylight had arrived, murky and gray, with a promise of snow to come. Susannah willed it fiercely to stay away until Will had been rescued.

Abby arrived with fresh coffee in hand, gave it to Susannah, and sank down beside her on the cot. "I just heard," she said, her eyes, filled with concern, on Susannah's face. "That boy who Jeremy went to see in the science lab? That Tim

Beech? He was one of the people taken to the blue area."

Susannah didn't even lift her head. Tim Beech was dead? Well, of course he was. If the Fire Captain's suspicions were correct, Tim had been sitting right in the middle of that explosion. How could he possibly be alive?

"I'm sure he never meant to blow up the building," she said, her voice so laden with fatigue, the words came out slowly, heavily. "Or to hurt anyone."

"No, I guess not." After a minute or two, Abby asked, "Susannah, are you okay? Where are your parents?"

"They went to the hospital to see how Jeremy is. Dr. Barlow is a good friend of theirs, and my mother said since things were winding down here, that's what she called it, winding down, they'd be of more help over at Emsee." Susannah let out a small sigh. "All they know about Will is that he's a paramedic and he's buried in there somewhere. They feel bad about that, but they don't know that if he doesn't come out of there alive, I'm not going to want to get out of bed in the morning."

"That's because you haven't told them how you feel about him," Abby said calmly. "I'll bet you haven't told anyone. Not even Will. *Especially* not Will."

Remembering the kiss, Susannah said, "Well, in a way, I have." She couldn't tell by the activity ahead of her if they were making any progress on that pile of rubble burying Will or not. "Abby, you've lived in Grant all of your life, too. Do you think if Will and I walked down the street together, maybe even holding hands, that people would hate us? Seeing us together, I mean?"

Abby thought for a minute. "Maybe. Some might. But, then, Sid and I get a lot of comments, too. People are curious about why a girl who can walk would be interested in a guy in a wheelchair."

"Does that bother you?"

"Nope. I'd rather be with Sid and put up with stupid comments than *not* be with Sid. That's all."

Susannah decided she couldn't see well enough. She stood up. She thought she saw a shovel waving in the air. "What if those comments threatened Sid in some way? Wouldn't that be different?" That *was* a shovel waving in the air. And there was another one, raised high in the air, swinging back and forth over someone's head, as if in triumph. *Not* in alarm, signaling for additional help. In *triumph*.

"The only difference it would make," Abby said emphatically, "is, I'd stick closer to Sid than ever. Anyone who wanted to make life miserable for him would have to go through *me*." She laughed as she rose to her feet. "And until I take off this extra ten pounds, they'd better not mess with me."

Sid came up behind them, asking, "What's going on?"

"You're right," Susannah told Abby softly, her bright blue eyes staring so intently at the pile of rubble, they began to tear up with the strain. Or maybe it was something else making them fill up suddenly. Because below the triumphantly waving shovels, a figure had appeared, one that hadn't been there before. It wasn't one of the volunteers, because there was no shovel in his hand, no flashlight, no pick. It was someone else. . . .

She took a step forward, then another, wanting to hope, but afraid. "You're absolutely right, Abby. No one has the right to tell Will *or* me who we can and cannot be with. Not even people who care about us and are concerned. Being afraid doesn't solve a single, solitary thing, does it? It just gets in the way. If you let it."

He had left the building now, was walking out into the open. His navy blue jacket was torn, almost shredded, his face was bloodied, and she could see that he was holding his left arm against his chest. His steps were none too steady. But when two of the workers moved to help support him, he brushed them away. Nothing doing, the gesture seemed to say, I'm walking out of here on my own steam. That was so like him. Strong, proud, fiercely independent Will. She'd bet anything *he* wasn't afraid.

Susannah began walking. All that blood on his face . . . did he have a head injury? How seriously had he been hurt? Struck down by those huge beams, buried under all that rubble, how could he even be alive?

But he was, oh, he was very much alive, and he was headed straight for her. He wasn't smiling, and she thought that was because he couldn't be sure it was okay to smile. Because he thought that maybe if he smiled, she wouldn't smile back. She couldn't blame him for being uncertain.

If she hugged him, the way she wanted to, right here in front of all these people, they would see . . . and they would know . . . and later on, when it was all over and they were all back in their homes, showered and in clean clothing and warm again, they would remember and they'd talk about it. They would say to their husbands or wives, "Could have sworn Will Jackson didn't stand a chance of coming out of there alive, but there he was, walking out of that mess like someone rising from the dead, and you'll never guess whose arms he walked straight into. There she was, hugging him as if she'd never expected to see him alive again. You'll never guess who it was in a million years."

And some of them, the ones Sam had told her about, would be angry. Very angry.

That's okay, Susannah thought, unable then to keep from breaking into a run, go ahead and get mad. But if you want to get to Will, you'll have to go through me.

And then he was there, and she threw her arms around him and held on to him as if she'd never expected to see him alive again, and he hugged her back.

Behind her, Abby broke into a grin and reached for Sid's hand.

epilogue

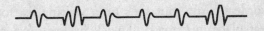

Susannah was carrying a bouquet of brightly colored balloons, Abby an enormous shopping bag, Sam a sports magazine, Kate a paperback joke book. Will, one arm in a sling because of a broken collarbone, his free hand locked in one of Susannah's, joked that he was empty-handed because his wallet had fallen out of his pocket when the beams hit him. It hadn't been recovered yet, so he was broke.

"You're always broke," Kate said as they walked down the hallway to Jeremy's room on the third floor of Grant Memorial. He had been transferred there from the ICU that morning. "Now all of a sudden you're going to blame that on falling beams?"

Will laughed. His face was dotted with scratches, there was a purple bruise beneath one eye, a patch of white gauze on one cheek, and stitches covered with clear adhesive tape on his chin. Every time Susannah looked at him, she winced. But she looked at him a lot, anyway, because she needed to keep reassuring herself that he was there, at her side, with no permanent damage.

"How's Margo?" Sam asked Kate just before they reached Jeremy's room.

"She's been transferred to Psych, to an eating disorders clinic. But she's on a waiting list for a great place in Canada. They'll fix her up. I saw her yesterday. She's still not eating, but she hasn't changed her mind about going, like I was afraid she would. Her parents are going ahead with the divorce, and she says she'd rather go to Canada than California."

Sam laughed. "I guess a lot of people feel that way about California. Me, I like the idea of sun and sand and surf."

"That," Kate said, "is because you look like the typical California beach boy. Even though you live in Massachusetts. How do you *do* that, Sam?"

"Smoke and mirrors, that's all it is. Where's your fireman friend?"

"Out fighting fires, I guess." But Kate smiled, thinking of the date she had with Damon that night. Nothing heavy, just a movie, maybe a burger. No big deal. She wouldn't even have bought that brand-new red sweater if it hadn't been on sale. A terrific bargain, really. She couldn't pass that up.

Jeremy was sitting up in bed, white gauze

around his head, but color in his cheeks. He hadn't been expecting them, and when he saw the balloons and gifts, he broke into a broad smile. "Man, I was just lying here thinking how lonely hospital rooms are," he said. "This is too cool! I thought you'd all be too busy to pop in here."

"We're never too busy for you, Jeremy, you know that," Abby said warmly. "Sid would have been here, too, but he's got physical therapy this morning, and I wouldn't let him out of it. I'm such a nag." She grinned. "But he loves me, anyway."

While Jeremy, a surprised, pleased expression on his face, looked over his gifts, Susannah, still holding Will's hand tightly in her own, glanced out the window, across campus. It was a bright, sunny morning, and she could see in the distance, past the well-landscaped grounds of Med Center, the forlorn, shattered Science building. The litter had been swept from the lawn, and the structure looked abandoned, though she knew, in fact, that plans to reconstruct the damaged floors were already on the drawing board.

If the explosion had taken place anywhere else, she thought to herself, even fifteen minutes further away from Med Center, more people would have died. Though no one could call the victims "lucky" to have been caught in the blast, they at least had had the good fortune to be injured so close to the finest medical complex in the country. That was something.

That, she thought, glancing up at Will and giving his hand a warm squeeze, was a *lot*.

An exciting excerpt from *Blizzard*,
Med Center #5, coming next:

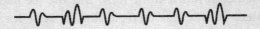

It began as rain. Not a warm, gentle shower, but a steady, chilly downpour that drenched streets and buildings and people unlucky enough to get caught in it. As the day progressed, temperatures plummeted. The rain began to freeze on its way down, turning to tiny ice pebbles that bounced off sidewalks and made sharp pinging sounds as they hit car hoods and metal drainpipes and tin roofs.

As darkness fell, every exposed surface in the city of Grant, Massachusetts, glittered with the thin, treacherous coating of ice. "Black ice," it was called, because it was difficult to see until you found your car or your feet or your bicycle wheels sliding across it out of control. Drivers cried out in terror as their vehicles spun wildly into one another. The air echoed with the sound of metal crunching against metal. Ambulances on their way to rescue accident victims found themselves fender-to-fender with other ambulances. Under the weight of the ice, powerlines snapped, hissing and crackling their way to the frozen ground.

When the city had become entirely coated with the deadly sheath of ice, snow began to fall. The rapidly thickening overcoat of white, too light and fluffy at first to make the ice safe, nevertheless hid it from view. But the ice hadn't melted. It was still there, laying in wait for its next victims.

A deceptively beautiful disguise, the snow continued to fall.

What could Sara have that a thief wants?

Every day Sara Howell faces mystery, danger ... and silence.

After Sara discovers the body of a museum security guard, her world turns upside-down: First her vacation condo is ransacked. Then her apartment back in Radley is robbed. What could the thieves be after, and how long before they come after Sara herself?

HEAR NO EVIL #4

Dead and Buried

Kate Chester

Coming soon to a bookstore near you.

Every day

Sara Howell

faces mystery, danger ... and silence.

HEAR NO EVIL

Kate Chester

❏BBW67326-2	**#1 Death in the Afternoon**	$3.99
❏BBW67327-0	**#2 Missing**	$3.99
❏BBW67328-9	**#3 A Time of Fear**	$3.99

Available wherever you buy books, or use this order form.

Scholastic Inc., P.O. Box 7502, 2931 East McCarty Street, Jefferson City, MO 65102

Please send me the books I have checked above. I am enclosing $_____ (please add $2.00 to cover shipping and handling). Send check or money order — no cash or C.O.D.s please.

Name_____Birthdate_____/_____/_____

Address_____

City_____State/Zip____/_____